*Acclaim For Other
Books By Dale Carlson*

*Girls Are Equal Too: The Teenage Girl's
How-to-Survive Book* (ALA Notable Book)

"Well-documented and written with intelligence, spunk, and wit."

— *The New York Times Book Review*

"Spirited, chatty, and polemical, *Girls Are Equal Too* gives a crash course in gender discrimination; from the history of women's subordination to self-empowerment today."

— *Publisher's Weekly*

"Clearly documented approach to cultural sexism in our society, Carlson reviews the image of women in the educational process, in the media, in dating and marriage."

— *School Library Journal*

Acclaim For Other Books By Dale Carlson

Where's Your Head? Psychology for Teenagers
(Christopher Book Award)

> "A practical focus on psychological survival skills… covers theories of human behavior, emotional development, mental illnesses and treatment."
>
> — *Publisher's Weekly*

> "Thoughtful discussion of different theories of mental and emotional development, mental illnesses, and their treatment, and common problems and their causes."
>
> — *The Science Teacher, National Science Teachers Association*

Stop the Pain: Teen Meditations

> "Five hundred years ago Dale Carlson would have been the village elder who, in the quietness and wisdom of her life, would have helped you see beyond the veil of the known."
>
> — *R.E. Mark Lee, Director, Krishnamurti Foundation, America*

STOP THE PAIN
Teen Meditations

STOP THE PAIN

Teen Meditations

Dale Carlson
Pictures By Carol Nicklaus

BICK PUBLISHING HOUSE   1999   MADISON, CT

Text Copyright ©1999 by Dale Carlson
Pictures Copyright ©1999 by Carol Nicklaus

Edited by Director Editorial Ann Maurer
Book Design by Jennifer A. Payne
Cover Design by Greg Sammons

All rights reserved: no part of this book may be reproduced or transmitted in any form or by any means, electronic or mechanical, including photocopying, recording, or by any information storage and retrieval system, without permission in writing from the publisher.

www.bickpubhouse.com

Library of Congress Cataloging-in-Publication Data

Carlson, Dale Bick.
   Stop the pain, I want to get off! : meditations for teens / Dale Carlson ; pictures by Carol Nicklaus.
      p.   cm.
   Includes bibliographical references and index.
   ISBN 1-884158-23-4
   1. Teenagers--Spiritual life. 2. Teenagers--Conduct of life.
I. Nicklaus, Carol, ill. II. Title.
BL625.47.C37   1999
158.1'2'0835--dc21   98-28757
                                                                 CIP
                                                                  AC

Distributed by BookWorld Services, Inc.
1933 Whitfield Park Loop
Sarasota, FL 34243
800/444-2524 or Fax 800/777-2525
941/758-8094 or Fax 941/753-9396

Printed by McNaughton & Gunn, Inc., USA

In Dedication

To all the young people everywhere who have answered, sometimes painfully, always honestly, our questions about their lives and feelings for so many years. And to their parents, teachers, and the librarians, who helped to organize groups for our dialogues.

To the late J. Krishnamurti (1895-1986), who taught us all the necessity of being free of any psychological authority, to look critically at ourselves as the source of our own suffering, the joy of going beyond the limits and prisons of those selves into freedom.

And to Ray Fisher, friend and philosopher, who opened the door.

For the new millennium.

BOOKS BY DALE CARLSON

FICTION:
The Mountain Of Truth
The Human Apes
Triple Boy
Baby Needs Shoes
Call Me Amanda
Charlie The Hero
The Plant People

NONFICTION:
Manners That Matter
Wildlife Care For Birds And Mammals

with HANNAH CARLSON

NONFICTION:
Living With Disabilities
Basic Manuals For Friends Of The Disabled:
    6 Volume Series
Where's Your Head?: Psychology For Teenagers

CONTENTS

Foreword by R.E. Mark Lee

Introduction
LIFE IS GORGEOUS: SO HOW COME I HURT?

Section One
WAKING UP

What Do We Want?	3
We Are All In Prison	9
How Many Selves Live (And Fight) In Your Brain? (Or, Who And What Are You?)	13
Thought And Insight: Intellect And Intelligence	19
War Or Meditation?	27

Section Two
MEDITATION

What Is Meditation?	43
The Many Ways To Meditate	49
When To Meditate, Where, With Whom	69

Section Three
PAY ATTENTION TO YOUR BRAIN OR IT WILL KILL YOU

Fear	*83*
Anger	*91*
Desire And Longing	*99*
Relationship And Isolation	*105*
Self-Awareness, Self-Knowledge, The Keys To Freedom And Power	*113*
Success And Failure	*123*
Loneliness, Depression, And Suffering	*129*
Sex	*137*
Money	*144*
Education	*147*
Love: Not Self, Dependency, Thought, Or Image	*155*
Truth, God, And Death	*163*

INDEX

BIBLIOGRAPHY AND SUGGESTED READING

DIRECTORY OF MEDITATION CENTERS, RETREATS, AND TEACHING GROUPS

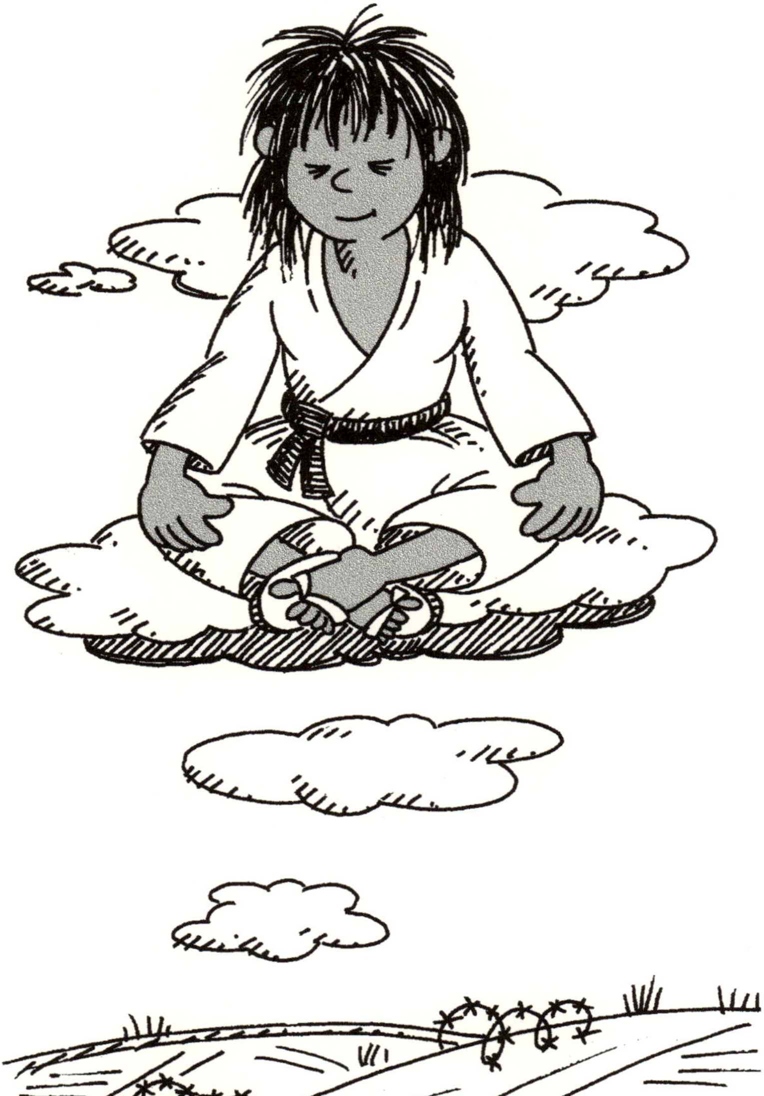

Foreword

There is some evidence that ancient people, our long ago relatives, lived in a meditative state most of the time. They were closer to nature, and they could communicate with animals and the forces of nature directly because there was no psychological disconnection between them and the rhythms of the earth.

Because there was no separation from nature, and because they were good observers outwardly and inwardly, they had fewer psychological problems.

Research suggests that the brain has been changing its potential and capacity for learning, memory, and simple work over the millennia. And it is *not* getting bigger, better, smarter. Actually, our capacities for complex calculations and sustained attention have diminished over the centuries. It does not take an anthropologist or a scientist to see why. In fact, you can see why in yourself – when you notice how much and how often you react to your environment, how dependent you have become, and how your psychological problems dominate your every waking hour. A book about living free of conflict, living happily, but making no false promises nor offering easy answers should interest everyone, particularly teens and young adults.

This is not a quiet book. It is a primer for learning about your brain and about life; both of which are moving and active most of the time. This book reflects that movement. And at the same time, there is a still point in the profound wisdom it represents. It points to the ancient ways of being quiet, and the ways of the ancients for being sane, healthy, and intelligent. The book says, "Wake up, you can do something in your life that will make you not dependent, but sane, free of conflict, and sensitive." Moreover, the beauty of being aware and awake is that it is free, it is not available in any store, it requires no prescription, and it has no side effects.

In short, this is all about what you did not learn in school, but it is what parents hope their children will discover. Five hundred years ago, Dale Carlson would have been the village elder who, in the quietness and wisdom of her life, would have helped you to see beyond the veil of the known.

She points the way, but is actually not telling you anything; in fact there is no real content to this book in that sense.

This book is simply a map of the territory of your life, and Carlson lets you fill in the facts and details. What she says is that there are no paths to follow, and that you have to discover the ways to truth for yourself.

R.E. Mark Lee, Director
Krishnamurti Foundation, America

Introduction

LIFE IS GORGEOUS: SO HOW COME I HURT?

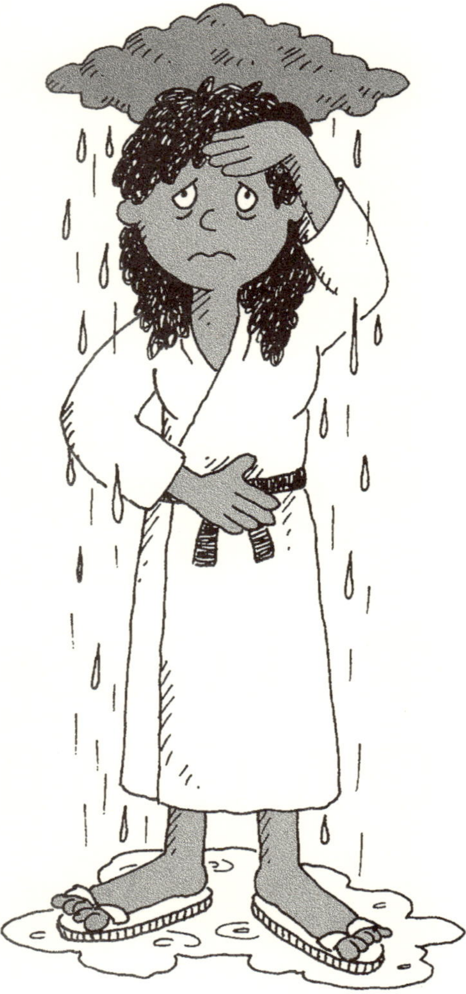

Life is Gorgeous:
So How Come I Hurt?

Life hurts. Even though we do what we think we're supposed to do, we still don't feel good inside.

Life is a glorious joy, too, of course, what with sunsets, music, falling in love. But it still comes as shock, especially in the teen years when so much is good and exciting, how much life can confuse and just plain hurt sometimes.

It hurts from fear, loneliness, from anger, despair. It hurts from being poor, or emotionally ill. It hurts from violence, whether in the street from crime, or at home or at school, from adults, or other kids. It hurts from failing, or being

xxii • Introduction

afraid to fail, at work, in class, at sports, on dates, in relationship. Depression, self-hate, rejection, envy, feeling different, left out, having to try too hard to keep up — the causes of hurt, of shame and pain and sheer terror come and go with every breath.

    The trouble is most of us never get taught to expect pain. We don't know where the pain is, where it comes from, and what to do about it. We never get taught that it isn't so much life, but our brains' reactions to life that cause the pain. It's the nonsense our brains have been stuffed with that mostly causes all the pain — what we're taught we are, what we're taught to want, what we're taught to hate and fear — and then our brains come up with solutions that cause even more pain. If your brain isn't going to kill you, you will have to pay attention to what it is doing, and how it is reacting to everything.

This is what meditation is, what the word means: to pay attention. *Stop what you're doing, sit down, shut up, and pay attention.*

What most of us do when our brains hurt, when we have mental pain, is try to fix the pain by escaping it: in drugs, alcohol, sex, violence, food, spending too much or gambling money, bone-breaking obsessions over another person or work or dangerous sports — anything to get high, get over, or numb out our feelings, our loneliness, our fears.

The trouble is, now we're stuck with two problems: with the original pain (it wasn't dealt with, so it's still there); and with the results of whatever was used as an escape (drugs, the wrong lover, AIDS, a jail sentence) as well. Again, it's a big shock how much life can hurt. But it's a bigger shock that we never got taught, along with reading, writing, computer technology, how to deal with emotional pain. And this is true whether we live in the projects or on Park Avenue, in the suburbs or the inner city, whether we are male or female, European American, African American, Chinese, from India or the South Seas. Personal and cultural differences are superficial. The whole human race belongs to the same species. We are as alike as ants. We all have the same brain.

Of course, we still only seem to use about 15% of it. We still don't know how its neural connections create either self or self-consciousness. We still don't know why our species is technologically ingenious enough to put someone on the moon and yet still point a gun or a plague at its own head. It's enough to make anyone nervous, if you think about it.

The point I'm making is, the human brain seems to have taken a wrong turn half a million or a million years ago. It *thought* it saw separate bodies instead of a connected universe, and invented separate and different selves instead of connected, nearly identical selves. This was the beginning of loneliness and fear and competition and killing, this mistake.

Society isn't THEM. It's all of us, you and me. Society is violent and insane. As we all share the same brain, the same consciousness, each brain affects all other brains. If even one of us changes, learns to understand and do away with mental suffering, grief, hurt, and fear that make for anger and violence, that change will affect all brains, all society, the minds of all of us.

So, it grows clear. Meditation is to pay attention to what is going on in your brain. It does not take an expert. Anyone can see that the brain has two main capacities: thought, which is the reaction of memory or stored knowledge; and observation. You can see by watching your own brain, we are either *thinking*, or we are *observing*. Meditation is not some strange, weird state of mind or standing on your head in a corner humming. Meditation is simply an awareness of these two capacities and how they work. It is paying attention to your reactions, what you like, what you don't like, the food, the culture, the habits of daily life and thought, attitudes about people, religion, country, family, everything you were brought up to. The whole point is to see all of this — and get beyond it. See what is actually going on inside and outside of you, not what you'd like yourself and the world to be, but actually what it is. The point is to transform our selves from being afraid and angry all the time. And to remember there is a reason for this: to the extent you change yourself, you change everyone around you. All our consciousnesses affect all of us.

Pain and hurt are part of life. They will happen. Somebody will die. We will fail, be rejected, feel lonely, left out, even in a crowd of friends. We will fear death or sickness, feel pity for our own life or the poor and sick of the world. It is thought's fear of pain and its effects on the very self thought has invented, that turns pain into long-term suffering.

Nobody tells us pain passes, that this year's agony won't even be a blip on next year's screen. Or if they do tell us, we don't believe it. Sometimes you have to stand the emotional blow, hurt for a while, before it goes away. This is as true of mental suffering as it is of physical suffering. Hurt feelings are no different than the cracked ribs caused by the lurch of a subway train or the wrong turn on skis. Anger, sadness, and fear are as physically based as any broken bone.

But there's a way to handle emotional pain so that it does pass instead of causing further damage. Use your brain, but use it in a different way. Too many of us have been taught that intellectual answers and explanations cure pain. What often happens, though, is that we're left with both the explanations *and* the pain. Instead of thought and analyzing which only prolong and often confuse, we'll go into the use of *insight, awareness of the brain's processes,* to get over emotional pain far more quickly.

So even if you're using drugs, alcohol, sex, food, shopping, gambling, self-mutilation, danger, romance, crime to get high enough, far away enough, to escape, cure, or deaden whatever bothers you — here's a different way to stop the pain, either now or later on.

This book is probably best read slowly, a little at a time. Because what you are really reading is not the book's words, but the book of yourself. And understanding yourself is not done once and for all. It is done constantly. Intelligent living is to understand every reaction as it happens, everything you do and say, every day. People who don't know themselves in daily life aren't cool: people who do know themselves are cool enough to know what they're doing all the time, not just for five minutes last Thursday.

Section One
WAKING UP

What Do We Want?

What is it we're all looking for? Most people want to be happy. We want to escape pain. We want to find some kind of inner peace so the yelling stops inside our brains. Most people want some kind of security, whether that means success, or at least freedom from failure, a loving and lasting relationship, the safety of having enough money, the fun of an endless supply of pleasure.

Why is it the brass ring always turns out to be hollow? You win the trophy, the boy, the girl, the lottery. Then comes the moment when you're standing somewhere by yourself, and you still feel empty. You get the feeling you're crazy, that there must be something wrong with you that nothing makes you lastingly happy, makes you feel safe. That's when the temptation comes to drop out, turn on, give in, run away. And that sometimes works for a while. But, if you are reading this, you must know that it's not a real solution. And when none of that works, what then?

Clearly, it's time to try something new, something different. If your car doesn't work, or threatens to run off the road, you have a look at the engine.

If your brain, like everyone else's brain, is trying to kill you, either with pain or the ways it invents of escaping, getting high to fight the pain, have a look at it. Watch your brain and its thoughts and ways, its habits, images, prejudices, desires, fears, its boredom and anxiety, and the troubles these cause. Meditation is not getting weird and holding your nose. Meditation is this watchful attention. Meditation itself will change the way you feel, show you the right way to go.

People have always asked:
- *What is the point of life?*
- *Is there a point to life?*
- *What is the meaning of me?*
- *Is there a purpose for me?*
- *How do I find out? Whom do I ask?*
- *Is there God, or something watching over me? If there's God, and if God is good, how come there is all this suffering — conflict inside myself; argument, crime, war, disease outside?*

My tremendous respect for the pain of teenagers is that the search for truth, the need for understanding in the midst of confusion are honest quests for the first time and sometimes for the last time in many lives. Pain makes most people glaze over, and bury deep, all concerns but superficial busyness as adults. For many people, adolescence may be the first and last time people ever want the truth.

There's a song that begins, "Why was I born, why am I living?" Most of us sing it, or at least mutter it under our breath.

We want approval.

We want love.

We want security and permanence, even after death, immortality for our precious selves.

We want to find out how to get these things.

We want to be permanently happy.

The fact is, you can be happy. You can end fear and loneliness, the inner torment and chaos and confusion that seems to be at its worst during our teens. Each of us can find out what's making us crazy and stop it.

Just not in the way we've been taught.

— • —

There is a difference between happiness and gratification. Perhaps you can find gratification but surely you cannot find happiness…it is a by-product of something else….

Study yourself, because what we are, the world is. If we are petty, jealous, vain, greedy — that is what we create about us, that is the society in which we live.
J. Krishnamurti
The First and Last Freedom

— • —

Your mind creates your universe.
Richard Alpert (Ram Dass)
Journey of Awakening:
A Meditator's Guidebook

— • —

You are the light of the world.
Jesus of Nazareth
Holy Bible, Matthew 5:14

— • —

Since all brains and the contents of their consciousness are pretty much alike, understanding your own brain is an excellent survival tool. You can keep yourself alive, and understand everyone else as well.

Also, since everything and everyone in the universe is connected to everything and everyone else, everything we understand, think and do matters, and we are all equally important in how we affect our common destiny.

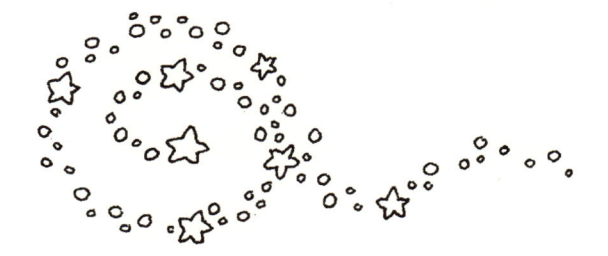

We Are All In Prison

The trouble with thought is, it thinks that's all there is in the brain. Thought is simply the response of memory, lots of memories, knowledge, the past, what was learned a long time ago, what was learned five minutes ago.

Thought also invents what we call our SELF, to give us a sense of security, of definition, so we have the feeling we're not falling apart all the time. Also, because the job of the brain is to protect the organism, to keep it alive, it makes and remembers images. Humans have no fur, claws, speed, or flight, to fight off other animals. We have thought. Thought creates images, and helps us remember not to hang around lions, to fear them. The trouble is, *thought is always creating images, remembering them, adding those images onto the original image of the SELF. We have lots of selves, actually. All those voices in our heads that keep arguing with each other, are all the different selves from all the different stages of our lives we've collected over the years.* Then the collective SELF, while it thinks it is keeping you safe, becomes a prison from which it is hard to escape. The SELF, with all its species/racial, cultural, gender, personal agenda memories, both conscious (open) and subconscious (hidden), becomes a house you live in behind locked doors. What you see through its windows is colored by all the information, prejudices, opinions, fears, pride, antagonism you've been handed for a couple of million years. Thought is the warehouse you've been handed. But it shuts you in as well as keeping others out.

Thought has its place, of course. You could not read this book, remember your name, speak, make science or medicine or music without thought.

But always remember, the brain does two things not just one. It thinks — and it understands. Thought (old stuff) and intelligence (right-now understanding, observation) are separate functions. Thought, often called intellect, makes science — intelligence tells you what is the right or wrong thing to do with it. Thought, intellect, is good for the technical part of life, but intelligence only will tell you about the right actions to take. The dumb person is not the one who doesn't know the contents of books, but the one who doesn't understand herself or himself, doesn't understand the proper place of thought, and therefore gives and gets pain.

Meditation is the discovery of the area of the mind that *isn't* thought — or the past, or knowledge. The area of the mind that *is* attention to what is going on *right now*.

What is going on right now changes all the time, like the river that flows on. You can't catch it and store it up, like knowledge. You just have to stay aware, awake all the moments of your life as it flows on.

As I said in an earlier book, *Where's Your Head?: Psychology for Teenagers,* "Understanding comes only through self-knowledge, which is awareness of one's total psychological process. Education, in the true sense, is this understanding of the ways of oneself and everyone else, not just information in books."

Leaving the cozy room you've created out of your thoughts can be terrifying — try changing your mind about anything, or try changing a single habit or addiction and you'll see how hard leaving anything familiar can be. And it won't work simply to redecorate, change the posters or the furniture, or exchange one old habit for another. You have to make a dash out the door into the sunlight to feel the difference between prison and freedom.

Prison is our old thoughts, and the accepted thoughts of society (really, the same thing, whether it's your parents' society, or your own peer society).

Escape now, before you get too used to it. This doesn't mean, break laws. There's no more freedom in real jail than mental jail. It means pay attention to your psychological attitudes. Are they all really yours? Are you stuck in them, trapped by ideas and behaviors you think you can't challenge?

How Many Selves Live (And Fight) In Your Brain?

Who and what am I?

Have you ever counted all the different voices in your brain that fight and shout at you all day, every day? Have you ever wanted to tell your brain just for five minutes to SHUT UP and LEAVE YOU ALONE!

All those voices are our different selves. Some are conscious and we are aware of them. Some selves are hidden; they speak to us from the unconscious part of our brains. The structure of the personality, its problems, its arguments with itself is based on everything that has been downloaded into the brain.

- animal, biological inheritance (we all have the basic animal urges for sex and aggression, the need to eat, eliminate, breathe, take shelter, stay alive)

- personal experience (the physical, psychological development of your own particular life)

- cultural inheritance (including sexual behavior, gender, color, religion, politics, family and social habits, prejudices and preferences)

The point is, we don't have ONE self, we have dozens. What we call ego or self is just a lot of tape-recorded announcements. Actually, this item we call *myself* is just a trick the brain plays, a group leader it invents, the mostly conscious part of the brain that is aware of what's going on around us.

Neurobiologists, brain specialists, have discovered that information is scattered all throughout the brain: *there is no little homunculus, no little person, no single "I" in there who makes decisions.* It just feels that way. But it's a group effort in the brain, and it has invented, in our civilization, the notion of "I." The sad part of this is, it makes us feel separate from other "I's" and is the cause of loneliness. Not all cultures, incidentally, encourage this "I" stuff, and more truly teach their children people are not separate identities, that the self is an inherited, communal affair. It saves everybody the trouble of murder and war to understand that if we kill someone else, we are killing part of ourselves.

You don't have to take anyone's word for this fact, that "you" are just a bit of fiction. Haven't you ever looked down your shirt and had the feeling there's nobody home? Haven't you ever said to yourself, "I have to pull myself together?" because you have the feeling you're all separate pieces? You're right on both counts. Haven't you surfed the perfect wave, thrown the perfect ball, gotten lost in a movie or a glorious sunset or the eyes of someone with whom you've fallen in love? There's no *me*, no *self* then, is there?, until "you" come back and run around inside your head collecting your pieces.

And then there's that hole everyone keeps trying to fill, with drugs or sex, with food or romance, with music and computers and cars, with ambitions and general busyness. Some people go into psychotherapy complaining of feeling empty. Even some therapists (happily, not the good ones) try to fill up people's empty spaces as if there were something wrong. What no one seems to teach us is that the hole is real, natural, and everyone has the same hole. It's supposed to be there, like an empty cup into which love and joy can spill from the universe. There's no room for anything beautiful and new if you have no space for it. And if you fill it up with junk, there's no room for life and beauty to pour in. That hole is the truth: there's simply no real "I" anyway.

16 • *Waking Up*

Meditation is understanding to good purpose. A hysterical preoccupation with my*self* is not the same thing as an awareness of the nature and ways of the *self* so it doesn't harm one's own person or anyone else's.

— • —

There is no self...the cause of all troubles, cares, and vanities is a mirage, a shadow, a dream.

Buddha
The Teachings

— • —

All of the insults to our narcissism can be overcome... not by escaping from them, but by uprooting the conviction in a "self" that needs protecting.

Mark Epstein, M.D.
Thoughts Without A Thinker

— • —

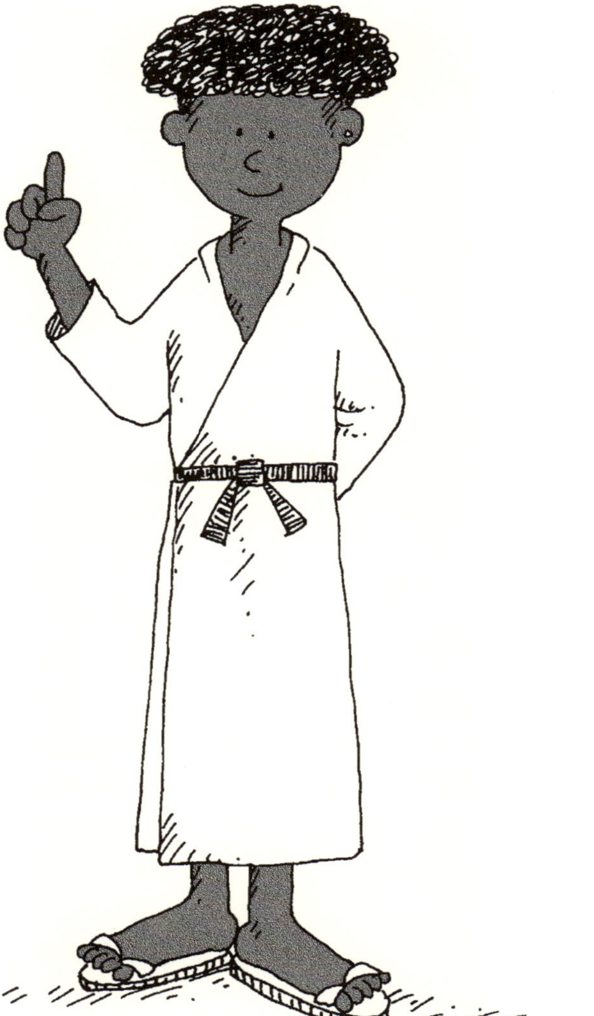

Thought And Insight: Intellect And Intelligence

The brain records, not necessarily accurately, what it experiences. It records your parents' voices and presences, your teachers' words, whatever nice or horrible thing your boyfriend or girlfriend or best friend said yesterday. It records what you see and hear on videos, the internet, television, the words to your favorite music. It records ball scores, whatever is cool to wear, the names of movie stars. It records, along with all the species information collected for a million years about what is good to eat, what is poison, how to climb a tree or crawl into a cave for safety, all the cultural and personal information collected by your group and by you personally.

There is a *South Pacific* song that says, "You have to be taught to hate and fear, you have to be taught from year to year, it has to be drummed in your dear little ear, you have to be carefully taught."

Interesting song.

Along with language, what to eat, and how to dress in your particular climate and civilization, what work is appropriate for your class, caste, sex, and position in life, you are also taught either by words or behavior to think the way your parents and friends think. That includes:

- what you are supposed to want
- what you are supposed to do with your life
- who you are supposed to know — and not know
- what is and isn't important (money, or success, or God, or popularity)

You know the rest.
Your personality is formed out of these groups of thoughts, each one an identity with its own reality: student to your teacher, child to your parents, sister, brother, buddy, lover, worker. Each has a social, sexual, cultural, intellectual, economic identity. It is easy to get lost in a particular identity in any given situation. Meditation, attention, intel-

ligence lets you pull back, give that piece of you some space, and see that it's only a fragment, and not the whole truth of you at all.

Then there are the thought patterns that are formed by the way society treats you. Society may say everyone is equal. Ask any young inner city person who lives in constant terror over with gangs, driveby shootings, drug dealers on corners, crime and violence in building halls at home and school, how fair society feels. Ask any young upwardly mobile suburban person whose parents' words never match their behavior. It's enough to make you schizophrenic when parents say one thing and do another. Many parents love their children, and many parents just say they love their children and are really too busy with their own affairs, their own fears and problems, their own pleasures, to pay attention to their kids. We all know whether we feel cared for or not. The problem also is, you can only teach others what you know yourself: if you can't feel affection, you can hardly pass it on, and thousands of generations of people making war, with their killings and terrorism, tell us there have been thousands of generations without affection.

Clearly, you can learn, accumulate knowledge, be a clever lawyer or business person, leader of a gang or a country, you can acquire all the skills and intellectual knowledge in the world — but this will not give you intelligence or skills in living your life happily.

This doesn't mean *not* to be a good student, doctor, mechanic, teacher, scientist, carpenter, businesswoman, or builder. It's important to learn technical skills, educational skills, to do what you do well. What we are talking about is not getting lost in these skills as identities. You can be a good anything without attaching self-importance to it. You can be helpful to people, this is a natural thing to do, without making a big deal out of it.

When you find yourself getting lost in any one of your identities, any one of your various selves (you can rate this by anxious feelings over whether you'll make the team, get the lover, get the grades), you can stop it like a bad dream by using meditation.

To think about this and analyze it, to get this verbally and intellectually, is a good first step. But it won't change anything. Intellect *gets it*. Insight, meditation, intelligence, *stops it*.

Stop here for a while. Listen to your brain for a day. Make a note on a pad every time you hear yourself, your selves, talking go you. List and identify all the different identities in your head. See if you can even take a shower by yourself,

Thought And Insight: Intellect And Intelligence • 23

without crowds of friends, parents, your own selves — all those different voices keeping you company or driving you crazy, however you like to look at it.

There was a sixteen-year-old boy who came to talk to me. He kept getting stoned. When he got high, he invaded houses in his neighborhood, and stole something. Sometimes it was a few dollars, sometimes a piece of jewelry, once even a stuffed dog. It was clear from the way he talked about his father, that his father was successful, wanted his boy to be successful, and used both excuses as reasons for his own busyness and how hard he was on his son. The boy felt his father's ambitions: he never felt his father's approval or love. Analysis made it obvious, the boy was stealing things to replace the love he did not get from his father. The stealing went on.

Insight made it clear nothing could replace his father's love. The stealing stopped.

Insight, not analysis, is the factor of change. Intelligence, not intellect, will change your daily life. Insight, intelligence, are just other words for attention and meditation. They can act on all the thoughts, all the fears you've inherited, all the prejudices, all the false values, and you can see the truth.

There's nothing wrong with hard work. You do not have to step on others to get where you're going. Or ignore loved ones because you are afraid of failure. Or get drunk, overeat, develop eczema because your levels of anxiety are insane.

There's nothing wrong with hanging out with people you like. But neither is it necessary to hate, fear, be mean to people you don't want to hang with.

There are all kinds of discrepancies in our lives: people think one way, talk another way, do and behave a third way altogether. You'll notice this if you watch for it.

Analysis can tell you why you do things. Intelligence will tell you to stop it if you're hurting yourself or others, or if what you're doing is getting you nowhere.

Most people only see and hear through the lens of what they already think. This is just reaction. Awareness sees beyond personal realities to the general or impersonal truth.

Meditation is not just about creating states of well-being: it is about destroying the belief in an inherently existent self....Insight arises when the thinker's existence is no longer necessary.

Mark Epstein, M.D.
Thoughts Without A Thinker

— • —

Meditative awareness is a vantage point from which you can focus on any event from various levels of reality. Take, for example, your relationship with your parents, spouse, or children. Your parent comes along and says something to which you immediately react and the parent in turn reacts to you. These are habitual reactions…in which nobody really listens; there is merely a mechanical run-off between people. If you are rooted quietly in your awareness, there is space….you see the reaction you would usually make. But you also see the situation in a variety of other ways…You might see that your parent is in fact…like you.

Richard Alpert (Ram Dass)
Journey of Awakening:
A Meditator's Handbook

— • —

War Or Meditation?

Most people, unless they are sociopaths, know right from wrong, good from evil, in the larger sense. Most of us are pretty certain killing friends for their bubblegum isn't nice.

But in the everyday matters of everyday life, who is going to tell you the right way to go, the right things to do, to have a happy life? Especially since, in the deeper sense, few people have discovered this in the 10,000 years of so-called civilization.

What people need is not guidance from the kinds of gurus or therapists with no more insight than anyone else. What people need is awareness, to be awake to the cause and effect of their behavior and its consequences.

The self is really a group of selves, arguing, in conflict, at war with each other. And it's clear if you act according to that inner warring self, you'll produce outer wars.

You can easily trace the path of anger and war. We begin by being angry at ourselves for failing to be a smart, brave, gorgeous, and successful as we think we should be. Our parents fight with us and each other because they are also more full of disappointment in their expectations of themselves and each other than they are full of affection. We fight with our friends for the same reason. We are all angry because we want things from ourselves first and then other people that we're afraid of not getting. All that anger has to go somewhere. We usually don't want to kill our selves, our own families and friends. So we take it out on being angry at neighbors, at people in the next town, at people of different colors and backgrounds and countries. War. It begins in and spills out from ourselves and home.

What if people could actually see and understand this? That war begins in the very structure of the self and its arguing needs and conflicts?

Might each person then handle conflict differently? Wouldn't there be different action?

So it seems clear that action must not come from self. It must come, it seems, from taking the trouble (and it is a lot of hard work) to understand that our conditioning, all that we're unthinkingly taught, all the desires, memory of fear, pleasure, pain, the need for approval and acceptance and so-called love — all this makes up thought that creates the warring selves.

The bad news is, the self isn't likely going to change, isn't going to go away. You can't take an ax to it. You can put it to sleep for a few hours with drugs, or romance or sex, but it always comes back to most of us. We know of a few, Jesus, Moses, Buddha, Lao-Tzu, Mohammed, Krishnamurti, and a whole lot of unsung women who were not allowed to speak in public — who didn't have egos or selves. The rest of us do.

So what?

You don't have to behave according to those egos, those selves. You don't have to obey them. You don't have to waste time trying to change yourself. **You can just change your behavior.** *Freedom from stupidity begins with changing behavior. What's interesting here is that as your behavior changes, the pathways in your brain are rewired and you become a different person. But the trick is to act your way into right thinking, since we can't seem to think our way out of a paper bag in our species except to invent the technology to get ourselves killed.*

A good beginning, in this watchful meditation, is to watch the self get angry.

Stop reading for a moment. Think of something or someone that makes you angry.

Pay attention to your body, the adrenaline rising, the face flushing, the head pounding, maybe the fists or the mouth or the stomach clenches. Can you just watch this happen to you and *do nothing?* Anger feels like a roller coaster ride. It will pass even if you do nothing. Interesting. Experiment with this. See if the next time you get angry, you can let it pass. See if your action is different, more appropriate, more effective. After all, lashing out at people you love isn't really satisfying in the long run, and you only end up feeling guilty. And as we've seen, pent-up personal anger only leads to collective war. So do see if next time you feel anger you can *just feel it and let it go by without doing anything about it.*

That's the reward of meditation. If your behavior is appropriate it works better than flailing your arms at the wind. Flailing leaves you always outnumbered and outrun by people more under control. It also leaves you exhausted.

Many people who study the human condition agree that *thought* is a less-than-accurate measure of the truth of anything. Scientists, metaphysical thinkers, philosophers have all begun to learn that the observer affects the observed; is, in fact, the observed. The "I" who is doing the looking, the imagining, brings along its own maps, processes, baggage, its own binoculars, its own lenses, through which it sees what it is looking at. Of course, this distorts the picture. In physics, it can be shown that the watched is changed by the watcher. In psychology, anyone can prove the same thing. This is why there are generally so many different stories told about the same event.

In his book *Reality & Empathy: Physics, Mind, and Science in the 21st Century*, Alex Comfort says, "Worlds are created by brains....At a simple level, bees, migratory birds, dogs...contain internal maps of their surroundings. Humans, who think abstractly, create more complicated...maps going beyond their own surroundings, to include the world, celestial objects, real and hypothetical beings, and the past and future as well as the present....Making world models is a familiar human activity."

In our culture, we call this activity religion or science. These are often ways of making up the world as we go along. Then we pass these ways along to others and to the next generations. If we can get them to believe us, it validates us and what we say. The trouble is that just because a million people believe something doesn't make it right **or** true. Remember when the ancient civilizations thought the world was flat? That women had no souls? That children were owned by their parents? That the sun went around the earth?

But as Richard Burdon Haldane says, "Nature [include human nature here] may not only be odder than we think, but odder than we can think."

Our perceiving system is the human brain. And this organ, we know, has its problems.

The point is that the observer is involved in everything observed. And the observer, the "I", the self, is limited to its own memories and information, its own fears, rages, desires, needs.

Happily, as we've pointed out, the human brain has another capacity: insight, or awareness, intelligence, whatever you like to call it. It may not be able to annihilate the self, but it certainly doesn't have to act according to it. Just because the self wants something, doesn't mean it has to have it. Just because *you* want something doesn't mean you have to give it to yourself. Just because you feel something, doesn't mean you have to make high mass out of it. Interesting freedom, isn't it? To be free of the bondage of yourself and all your voices is a lovely, happy way to live.

To go back to those questions at the beginning of this section that people always ask about the point and the purpose of life, what the Dalai Lama, the exiled spiritual leader of Tibet, says, is that it is *to be happy.*

This is trickier than we know. Being happy doesn't mean getting lost in some superficial pleasure that will only pass. It means staying awake, aware, all the time:

- so we don't turn temporary pain into long-term suffering

- so we understand that thought has its proper place and we do not let it spill over from the technological arena into the psychological arena

- so that we see the world and its people with new eyes every moment, not through the filter of the past

- so we can see that suffering depends on how we react inwardly to outside events, not on the outside events themselves (these can cause some pain, but we don't have to keep suffering over pain, the past)

- so we can see it's our own brains with their fears, angers, cruelties, memories that cause the suffering, not the gods (a volcano is the earth burping, and it's true that if people's houses are in the way, they get trashed, but this is no more personal than you or me burping and there's no point in confusing nature's activity with the extraordinary glory of the universe many people call God)

War Or Meditation? • 35

1. Thought, the response of memories, with its knowledge, the contents of consciousness and intellect — is the PAST.

2. Insight is always perception in the NOW.

3. Thought is TIME — not time by the watch or the time it takes to get to Pittsburgh — but psychological time as past, and future.

Insight is now.
You can always have insight.
It is always now.

The Dalai Lama is right about the purpose of life is to be happy, to feel joy (remembering that happiness and just pleasure are not the same thing). People breathe out what's inside them. If people are full of misery, that's what they give off. And the world does not need any more bad breath.

— • —

Even a mind that knows the path
Can be dragged from the path:
The senses are so unruly.
But he [who] controls the senses
And recollects the mind...
I call him illumined.
>   translated by Swami Prabhavananda
>   and Christopher Isherwood
>   The Song of God: Bhagavad-Gita

— • —

We have what we seek. It is there all the time, and if we give it time it will make itself known to us.
>   Thomas Merton
>   New Seeds of Contemplation

— • —

— • —

The thinker is the thought…In his thought, the thinker is revealed. The thinker through his actions creates his own misery…. This is the rock wall against which you have been battering your head, is it not? If the thinker can transcend himself, then all conflict will cease: and to transcend he must know himself.

J. Krishnamurti
The Book of Life, edited by R.E. Mark Lee

— • —

Meditation is not a matter of trying to achieve ecstasy, spiritual bliss or tranquility, nor is it attempting to become a better person. It is simply the creation of a space in which we are able to expose and undo our neurotic games, our self-deceptions, our hidden fears and hopes.

Chogyam Trungpa
The Myth of Freedom

— • —

The truth shall make you free.

John VIII, 32, The Bible

— • —

Waking up gives you peace, freedom, and joy. Not too bad a trip.

Section Two
MEDITATION

What Is Meditation?

You already know what meditation is. It's that state of being out of yourself when the sky, the wave, the game, the lovemaking, the ocean is perfect. It's that state when there is no separation between you and another, you and the sky or wave, the game or the sunlight. We've all had these moments. These are the moments when there is no feeling of separation and loneliness, and you feel at one with the entire universe. Meditation is what happens when thought, with its self, and its problems, stops, and there is only attention. Most of the time, there is the feeling of calling out to another, to the world, from inside the box, the house of the self, we all live in. We all try for intimacy, with hugging, with talk, with sex, with games, but there's still the sensation, even among friends, even at a family party (sometimes especially on those occasions when everybody is trying hard to pretend unity) when there's only a black hole and no real ground under your feet at all.

The bliss of meditation is connection, the end of separation, of black holes, of the terror of total loneliness. With the art of meditation, you can stop isolation whenever you like. Artificial means like LSD or hypnosis are only temporary, and addictive, and eventually totally destructive. Meditation is natural to us all. We've just never been shown the way. The way can be as simple as sitting down, back straight so you can breathe properly, and shutting up. Watching the breath coming in and going out, watching thoughts and letting them go by instead of getting lost or crazy in them. This exercise works better than any artificial means, works most of the time, and leaves no destruction in its wake.

We've all been in this silence. Sometimes, it makes us panic and rush right back into the old, familiar room. We can learn to tolerate the freaking out until it passes and stay out there, out of the room for longer periods of time.

Meditation is found in silence. This doesn't mean just turning the music off. Or just not talking to other people or yourself. It is the gap between thoughts, total attention when the self is absent. Krishnamurti says it best, to my mind.

— • —

Meditation is one of the most extraordinary things, and if you do not know what it is you are like the blind man in a world of bright color, shadows and moving light. It is not an intellectual affair, but when the heart enters into the mind, the mind has quite a different quality; it is really then, limitless, not only in its capacity to think, to act efficiently, but also in its sense of living in a vast space where you are part of everything.

Meditation is the movement of love. It isn't the love of the one or of the many. It is like water that anyone can drink out of any jar....And a peculiar thing takes place which no drug or self-hypnosis can bring about: it is as though the mind enters into itself...In this state there is complete peace — not contentment which has come about through gratification — but a peace that has order, beauty and intensity....The soil in which the meditative mind can begin is the soil of

> *everyday life, the strife, the pain and the fleeting joy. It must begin there, and bring order, and from there move endlessly....You must take a plunge into the water, not knowing how to swim. And the beauty of meditation is that you never know where you are, where you are going, what the end is.*
>
> J. Krishnamurti
Meditations

— • —

Meditation is not separate from daily life. It is not just going off into a corner, saying some magic words, mantras or prayers, and coming out to behave the same horrible ways. It is paying attention to everything you do in daily life, everything you say, how you behave, what you are thinking. It is taking time for walking or sitting in silence so your life can be reflected in the pool of that silence. In silence, the universal intelligence, what some call the still small voice, can be heard, sharing truth with you, giving you the right actions, the right moves, how to handle your feelings and problems. Only in this silence, when there is no interference from all the voices of the selves, can you hear without the static of all your brain's tape-recorded announcements. In silence, oneness with everything is possible, and an end to fear, anxiety, loneliness. It is like holding hands with love. It is the discovery that there isn't good luck or bad, there's just life.

This ability for meditation and silence is not just the property of priests and ministers, yogis and rabbis, shamans, saints, and other holy women and men. We all have this ability in our brains. You've been there often enough to know this absence of self already, in moments of crisis when someone else needs you, when a burst of energy is required, when you've suddenly had the feeling of coming back to yourself with a thud after dancing, or music, or TV or a movie. Coming down, coming back, means you've been away. Right?

Now discover how to do this anytime, any place, all the time, in all places.

The Many Ways to Meditate

There are helpful ways to begin to meditate. First you need to quiet your brain and body so you *can* meditate. There are lots of meditative practices from chanting to mantras, from breath-counting to yoga, dance, martial arts forms. The choice of ways to quiet the body to quiet the mind are various and many. For some people, simply reading and following what is suggested in this book or other meditation books such as those listed at the end are enough to get started. For others who are more active or prefer company, want variety or further teaching or dialogue, there are retreats, camps, centers, abbeys, foundations, and schools, also listed at the end of this book.

None of these are necessary. You can simply be aware of what you like to do in your own life and begin there. With reading Krishnamurti or the *Bible*, Buddhist teachings, the Hindu Gita, the poems of Maya Angelou, the prose of W.E.B. du Bois, or for those too active to sit for long, with kung fu, karate, tai chi, sufi dancing. Turning on with your own mind and body is a high better than turning into stoners and drinkers. The author has done them all, and can vouch for this scrap of sooth.

List of some ways into meditation, to be described in detail in the following pages:

1. Sitting meditation.

2. Walking or moving meditation: kung fu, tai kwon do, karate, tai chi, hatha yoga, Japanese tea ceremony, cooking food, gardening.

3. Breathing practice, either prana yoga or Buddhist zen practice for example.

4. Relaxation techniques.

5. Singing, chanting.

Mantras and prayers, rosaries and davening, puja, Buddhist, Hindu, Native American offerings and chants, Catholic masses and Jewish or Protestant services, incense, candles, pipe ceremonies, prayer wheels, ancestor and nature worship — anything, everything can help to quiet the brain's noise. *But the whole point is eventually to integrate the mindfulness of sitting and moving meditations into watching yourself in everyday life.* So you can lose the anxiety in calmness. So you can wear the world as a looser garment instead of a hair shirt. So you can acquire duck oil, and the hurts of daily life can roll off your back instead of jabbing you in the throat, groin, and solar plexus.

Meditation is *not* a toy. It has side effects.

- extra energy, physical, emotional, sexual

- or tiredness at first (just the initial relaxation of your nerves and muscles)

- resistance (this may take the form of boredom, and boredom is just a form of resistance, in the beginning, a "why-am-I-doing-this" voice running frantically around your brain making you feel silly as well as bored) — pay no attention, it will go away as the lovelier effects take place)

- anxiety, nervousness, difficulty just physically sitting still in the beginning happens often to athletes, female and male, and more often to younger males — don't worry, stay with it, your system will eventually quiet down

- ecstasy, real highs

- hallucinations, aural or visual (you may at first be visited by old memories in the form of demons, you may feel a haunted terror) — after all, a different set of chemicals run around a meditative brain that may create images, sensations, smells, sounds

- speed (you may feel your brain speeding up, your heart pounding, your nerves jumping)

- CLARITY, INSIGHT, CONNECTION, COMMUNION, INNER PEACE AND HARMONY — these are the greatest side effects of all

SITTING MEDITATION

You can begin meditation right now, if you would like to try the experiment. First, walk around your life until you find a quiet place. The front porch. Your bedroom. The bathroom. The woods, or under a tree in a city park. A corner of a garage, a wrecked car in an abandoned lot. The beach is nice, an alley will do. Anywhere you can be alone and quiet, lower your eyelids, and go inward, inside yourself. A patch of sky, a bit of green, a ray of sunlight, something not man-made is good to be near. A lit candle is fine. The moon or sun is better. The light, the bit of sky, or something green and alive are an extra benediction. They are not absolutely necessary. Even external quiet and solitude aren't totally necessary.

What is necessary is to sit somewhere, and to sit quietly. Now, SIT.

Sit in a chair, on the stairs, on the floor. Sit with your back straight, not rigid, shoulders down. You can sit cross-legged or in lotus position, or if you are on a higher seat, have your feet on the floor. Do not lean against a wall. You cannot carry a wall with you through life to lean on. Sit as if your butt and your back were a comfortable and supportive chair. Once you learn to sit well, you'll return to sit in your body like a familiar and welcoming chair. Relax. *Relax, not collapse.*

Keep the body, even the eyes, still. You can close them. Or you can lower your eyelids and focus them on a spot six feet in front of you. In this stillness lies the sound of truth, what some people call 'the still, small voice,' and others call god or the universe — and the greatest high you have ever known. It is in this stillness that personal troubles and the troubles of the world fade away.

Breathe, and keep the attention to the breath. When your brain wanders off, bring your awareness back to the breath. Watch your thoughts as they follow each other through your brain, but don't let any of them drag you down roads like wild horses. In one form of Buddhist sitting meditation, the breath is breathed in to the count of five, and let out slowly to the count of ten. In another, ten in-and-out breaths are counted and the count starts again. If you lose your place, it means your attention has wandered. Start again. In yoga meditation practice, eyes are closed, or attention is on a spot six feet in front of you, perhaps on a lighted candle, on a loved object, on simply a stone. To lose sight of the object results in a loss of concentration. The whole point of any practice is actually not meditation itself, but to quiet the mind so thoughts slow down and finally stop and the silent gaps between thoughts lengthen. *The trick here is not to avoid thoughts or make an effort to control thoughts. The trick is to watch your thoughts instead of thinking them, to see what you think about so you know what concerns you, not to analyze those thoughts.* Just let the thoughts happen — if you don't bother them, after a while they won't bother you.

The trick here is, there is no trick. Do nothing. Have no expectations. Do nothing. There is nothing to do. JUST SIT. Sit for only four or five minutes to begin with. See what happens. Eventually, sit for longer periods of time, 20 minutes, even 40 minutes. Again, just see what happens.

— • —

The state of mind that exists when you sit in the right posture is, itself, enlightenment.... There is no need to talk about the right state of mind. You already have it.

Shunryu Suzuki
Zen Mind, Beginner's Mind:
Informal Talks on Zen Meditation and Practice

— • —

— • —

The ultimate aim is to bring mind and spirit together with the body in perfect unison.

Ron Van Clief
The Manual of the Martial Arts:
Introduction to the Combined
Techniques of Karate, Kung-Fu,
TaeKwonDo, Aiki Jitsu for Everyone

— • —

Examples of trains of thought that might pass through your mind, remembering that some thoughts will be deep, some passing, some light, some frightening, some funny. All these thoughts are yours, are you. They might go something like this:

- math test tomorrow, English paper Monday, soccer practice, find team sweater
- what shall I wear to the party?
- bring odometer for run
- kill girlfriend for flirting with my buds last Saturday
- where are you when I need you, god?
- back hurts, bod needs help
- I'm bored, so why was it I'm sitting here?

The Many Ways To Meditate • 57

- is sex to boyfriend just sex or does he love me like he says?

- I gave her my class ring, why doesn't she trust me?

- what will happen to my brain if I go on experimenting with drugs? what will happen to my popularity if I don't?

- does the team still like me after last game's goofs, or am I just kidding myself?

People have reported altered states of consciousness, paranormal visions, half-forgotten memories, terrifying childhood nightmares and experiences, demons, ringing in their ears, at first. People have also reported boring lists of tasks, possessions, errands. All of this is *you*. Nothing comes at you from outside.

> *I will recognize whatever appears as my projection and know it to be a vision...I will not fear the peaceful and wrathful ones, my own projections.*
>
> Chogyam Trungpa
> The Tibetan Book of the Dead

As you sit, fantasies, fears, memories, thoughts continue to flow through your brain. Whether you have done yoga postures, readings, focussing, breathing to quiet the body, you have now stopped, you are quiet. You are not hanging on to any thoughts or ideas, you are letting them go by, watching them like pooh-sticks floating down a stream. This is meditating. You're doing it. If you grab at any of the fantasies or memories, or you analyze or problem-solve, you are just thinking again. Let go again, and again you're meditating. Over and over your mind may get caught on your thoughts, a sound, a plan. Just keep letting go and bring your attention back to your quiet sitting, your breathing.

This is the beginning of meditation, of the silent mind.

It's the best way in the world to know yourself — to see what's on your mind. Not get involved with it, just see it. What's going on with you will become clear. And this self knowledge is the key to freedom from the suffering the self causes. Attention, it turns out, not control, is the way to change one's life.

As you get more practiced, you can bring any problem to your meditation. Not to think about, solve, or analyze. You can just drop it into your silence, like a quarter in a slot, *and listen for, not think about, the answer.* You can find out what interests you to do with your life, what to know about anger or fear, how to handle situations, by asking the universe a question, and in your altered state of consciousness, learn the art of listening for what comes to you.

Other people have been here before you for thousands of years. Many of their writings are listed in the back of this book, as well as throughout.

WALKING OR MOVING MEDITATION

Yoga. Martial arts. Surfing. Skate boarding. Biking.

Gardening. Cooking food. Making tea. All these slowly, ceremoniously.

Walking. Chanting. Dancing. Singing. Prayer. Communing with nature.

Devotions. Visualizations. Mantras.

Mindfulness in everyday life.

Mindfulness is doing whatever you do with complete attention, so it actually happens to you. If your own life and what you do every day doesn't happen to you, what will? We live so much of our lives mechanically. There's the experience we all have of walking or riding somewhere and arriving without knowing how the time passed. It went by without our being conscious of it. We don't want to arrive on our deathbeds, look back at our lives, and say, "What was that?"

Eat mindfully. Walk mindfully. Lie down, get up, speak mindfully, with full attention to what you're doing. It will make everything in life more meaningful.

All of the above physical paths are wonderful preparations for the inner silence of meditation. You will discover there isn't a need to think all the time, have opinions all the time, and since there isn't a need, you can try not having any sometimes. It's very difficult not to like this, dislike that, want this, not want that. To center yourself:

- Row a boat.
- Run a mile.
- Dance for twenty minutes.
- Play a guitar or a flute.
- Chant or sing, say a mantra or prayer. For an excellent variety of these, read Ram Dass' *Journey of Awakening: A Meditator's Guidebook.* Read the *Bible,* St. John of the Cross and other saints, Thomas Merton, the *Bhagavad Gita,* the *Upanishads,* the

Koran, Buddha's *Dhammapada* (Teachings), Lao-Tzu's *The Way of Life (The Tao)*, *The I Ching*, African and Native American teachings. I like to remember always, though, what St. Therese of Lisieux said: "I felt it better to speak to God than about him." And that a silent openness to the universe is as much prayer as a dialogue with god.

- Read: especially read the way great minds and religious philosophers and teachers, and particularly Krishnamurti among them, wrote about meditation. Try Krishnamurti's *Total Freedom: The Essential Krishnamurti*.

- Do ten kung fu or yoga exercises, or twenty minutes of calisthenics. If you don't know any of these arts, get Richard Hittleman's *Yoga: 28 Day Exercise Plan*, with over 500 step-by-step photographs, Ron Van Clief's *The Manual of the Martial Arts: An Introduction to the Combined Techniques of Karate, Kung-Fu, Tae Kwon Do, and Aiki Jitsu for Everyone*, also with photographs of forms and techniques.

- Do zazen, sitting exercises. Read *Zen Mind, Beginner's Mind, Informal Talks on Zen Meditation and Practice* by Shunryu Suzuki.

- Write or read poems, particularly by poets (like the great African American poet Langston Hughes) who understand human pain, the kind that especially torments adolescence.

— • —

Because my mouth
Is wide with laughter
And my throat
Is deep with song,
You do not think
I suffer after
I have held my pain
So long?

Langston Hughes
The Dream Keeper

— • —

Meditation may even go on in your sleep.

— • —

A dream is the answer to a question we haven't yet learned how to ask.

Fox Mulder
The X-Files

— • —

Or in the silence that is
a form of prayer.

— • —

The fruit of silence is prayer.
The fruit of prayer is faith.
The fruit of faith is love.
The fruit of love is service.
The fruit of service is peace.

Mother Teresa
Missionary of Charity

— • —

The ability to pay attention, to be in a constantly meditative, aware state of mind will help you determine whether what you are being taught, what you hear, and see, and witness is true or false. After all, we are all subjected to what Robert Persig calls in his book *Zen and the Art of Motor-*

cycle Maintenance, "mass hypnosis—in a very orthodox form known as education."

Whether walking, eating, reading, thinking, moving, or sitting, simply be aware that walking, eating, reading, thinking, moving, or sitting is happening.

— • —

Just let things happen as they do. Let all images and thoughts and sensations arise and pass away without being bothered, without reacting, without judging, without clinging, without identifying with them...That's what we are—a sequence of happenings, of processes, and by being very mindful of the sequence, of the flow, we get free of the concept of self.

Joseph Goldstein
The Experience of Insight

— • —

What you discover in meditation is that events are simply the result of cause and effect, even if we can't always figure out the causes or can't see far enough ahead to know all the effects. What a tornado is *not*, however, or a broken leg or an ended love affair, is an act of a personally vengeful god who's got it in for you. (Try not to confuse acts of physical nature with the intelligence and order of the universe.) Meditation will give you insight into the causes of your troubles — in your choices, your selves, your conditioning, your attachments, your ghosts and voices. The bad news is that it is usually ourselves that cause the trouble. The good news is, it's easier to fix yourself than some unknown, uncontrollable power.

As we've said, while a lot of being in your teens is good, fun, exciting, another part of it is pure torture, outer conflict, inner chaos, and total confusion. With some experimenting, you may find meditation is an excellent substitute for suicide in problem-solving.

Where To Meditate, When, With Whom

Y ou really don't have to go anywhere to meditate except inside yourself. But sometimes it's a nice change to leave the noise and dailiness, even the quiet corner where you usually sit to ponder over your life, and go where others are doing the same thing. There are meditation centers, retreats, monasteries, convents, yoga groups, zen temples, Christian, Jewish, Moslem, Sufi, Native American, African American, Latino, Buddhist both Tibetan and Japanese, meditation centers, martial arts schools, meditation schools of all kinds, YMCA, YWCA, camp groups, retreat houses, seminaries, institutes, and foundations without end to choose from all over the country, all over the world. You can go to India. You can sit in your back yard. Some facilities are listed at the back of this book, and you can find nearby centers in your telephone book. Ask your local rabbi, minister, priest, yoga or martial arts teachers as well.

The point is, *there are no secrets here, no magic rituals, no special places, no experts.* It's just people, sitting, going inside themselves, giving themselves space to understand the workings of their own self which is the same as other selfs, reading their own book of life, so very much like everyone else's book of life.

The whole point of meditative silence, of giving the mind the space to go over the details of your life is that you are able to learn for yourself whatever you want to know about. You can't live on someone else's truth second hand: you have to discover it for yourself. In Alcoholics Anonymous it is said, you can't get sober on someone else's sobriety — you have to stop drinking yourself. This is true revolution: to learn life for yourself. Rebellion is just a negative blueprint, a reaction to someone else's truths, not freedom.

And the business of truth is *not* a matter of doctrines and rituals, or even always the vast business of god and the cosmos. Truth has to do with everything in everyday life. With a revolutionary attitude of finding out for yourself, you can even discover whether you're really hungry at dinner, really love sports or the computer or the stuff your friends like, or whether you've simply been told dinner is what people do at six o'clock, it's abnormal not to watch football or pant over a rock star. What other attitudes and habits are part of your psychological inheritance, your educational system? We have been told what to think instead of being taught to think for ourselves. Prejudice, greed, ambition, escape through drugs, drinking, devouring other people's lives, dependence on approval, all of this is taught along with history, shop, home economics, math, bed-making, dish-washing, and tooth-brushing.

Part of the problem even in talking about meditation is that this is another preconception we've been taught, like religion, or god. There is no gap between us and the universe or god or religion or meditating. It is as natural to the human heart and psyche to think about and doubt and struggle with these matters as it is to breathe. Matters of the human spirit are not a question of being "good" or "nice" (I've known some perfectly nasty spiritual people, and some perfectly charming gangsters) or even of giving money or volunteer time to those for whom life has been less kind — this is a natural activity, no great virtue. And don't get the idea that monks and nuns don't struggle and doubt and question: they do. Just like the rest of us.

Meditation, silence in the presence of the universal connection, is available to anyone. It is simply a question of self-examination and behaving ourselves so our lives have meaning and beauty and purpose instead of just going to hell in a handbasket.

What this is about is a warning: most books, teachings, lectures, groups, sects are more interested in proving they are right and the only path, that the leaders are something special, than with showing everyone how simply to sit, go inward, and listen for themselves to what comes to them.

Truth is a pathless land.

Why do you want to be students of books instead of students of life? Find out what is true and what is false in your environment with all its oppressions and its cruelties, and then you will find out what is true.

J. Krishnamurti
The Book of Life: Daily
Meditations With Krishnamurti
Edited by R.E. Mark Lee

The whole point is that we must see with our own eyes and not accept any laid-down tradition as if it had some magical power in it. There is nothing magical which can transform us just like that....There is a great attraction to the short cut.

Chogyam Trungpa
Meditation in Action

— • —

Beware of false prophets.

Matthew 7:15
The Bible, New Testament

— • —

All of that being said, and with the understanding that outer forms and disciplines, rituals and exercises are not the point, it can be wonderful fun and very healthy to take physical yoga classes in a place like Kripalu or a local yoga center with a good teacher. Yoga has been, after all, the grandparent for thousands of years on which calisthenics for sports, gym exercises, military drill, and aerobics are based. It can be a tremendous experience to do sitting meditation in a group in a Buddhist zendo, a Christian meditation center, a Native American vision quest. It is lovely to go on retreat with a church or camp group, to join a chanting or singing or prayer group, spend contemplation time at a monastic retreat or spiritual center of any sect or denomination of any religion. You don't have to subscribe to beliefs or enlist in religions or sects to enjoy the quiet of sacred places.

You can do relaxation techniques, yoga exercises, tai chi by buying a video as well as going to a class. Invite a friend or two over and start your own group. Proper breathing to oxygenate your brain and relax the muscles of your body is important. Eating healthfully is important. Cleaning up your life a little by watching what you watch on TV, what you do with your time. WATCH WHAT YOU HAVE ATTACHED YOUR SENSES TO AND SEE HOW HARD IT IS EVEN TO GIVE UP ONE VIOLENT PROGRAM OR YOUR POTATO CHIPS.

Don't fool yourself that you can imitate someone else's act. Your life cannot be borrowed from someone else any more than a tattoo. Anything you do, from giving up eating dead animals to saying no to the next drink or act of meanness, can be hard. But it's easier if you do it from your own conviction that just to wear a temporary halo that belongs to someone else.

As you begin to see that some of your old habits are just holding you back from the life you want, you may find, sadly, that your friendships change, even your relationships with your family change. Not so much that you reject them, but they may reject you for moving ahead with your life.

— • —

Your kinsmen are often farther from you than strangers.
Ali

Maxims of Ali

— • —

But deepening your meditation and getting on with a kinder life are the best tools for fighting the most common horrors of adolescence, the three D's — depression, drugs, drinking. The rates of adolescent suicide prove the presence of these. A recent article in *Twist* magazine describes a chain of suicides in a high school in Michigan, that led the kids to call their school "Suicide High." The school was full of eerie vibes, the young people said, too many of them feeling sad, hopeless, worthless, wanting to be anywhere but where they were. A "Surviving Depression" article in *Teen Voices* magazine points to the same problem.

Obviously, sitting around and breathing isn't the cure. It's what you find out about yourself and life while you're sitting around breathing that's the cure. Everybody has to learn someday that the world isn't the way we think it is, solid and forever. Rather than solid, it is fragmented, broken into atoms and molecules, and impermanent, always changing and in flow like a river. It's easier to learn this now while you're young instead of when you're old, rigid, and it's too late to change much. There's no point in trying to hold your arms around a world you've made up, hoping to keep it together: it's like hugging sand.

Lose control. Not of your behavior. Just the world, the future, other people, and all the other weather you are powerless over. We keep acting as if we're not going to die. We are. Make life count.

We ourselves make up our own universe. Even when bad things happen, we make up our own reactions to them. Meditation doesn't mean do nothing. It doesn't mean sitting around drifting. Whether in sitting silence or in action, it simply means WAKE UP AND PAY ATTENTION!

— • —

Calmness of mind does not mean you should stop your activity. Real calmness should be found in activity itself.

There is no particular way in true practice.

Shunryu Suzuki
Zen Mind, Beginner's Mind

— • —

Jesus spoke of compassion. Buddha taught freedom, not of, but from the self. The Indian saint Kabir and the Western saint Therese yearned for the love of and connection to god. Lao Tzu and Confucius talked about right living. It's all the same. When 'me' is here, life is small, full of fear, often vicious. When 'me' is not there, and there's only attention, the world opens wide.

When To Meditate, Where, With Whom • 79

As always, it's a question of turning the eyes into windows, not mirrors.

Section Three

PAY ATTENTION TO YOUR BRAIN, OR IT WILL KILL YOU

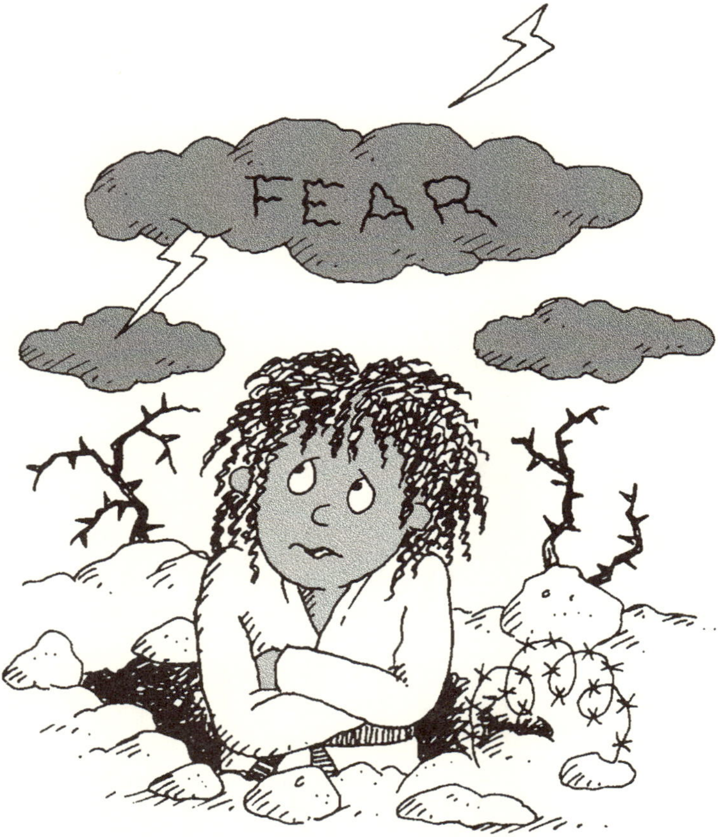
FEAR

Fear

We are all afraid of one thing or another all the time. The whole job of the self is to protect itself, just as the whole meaning of life is to stay alive. We are all mostly interested in ourselves, in our lives, our affairs, our prestige, our satisfactions (even helping others can be self-satisfying). Getting what we want out of life. What we are afraid of is not getting we want or losing what we have. So we fear death, of the body, of our selves, of our egos. We fear loss of reputation, popularity, the people and things we depend on, our friends, money, jobs, a place in the world. We fear darkness, loneliness, inner emptiness. We fear authority, certain people. Our problem is that we are ashamed to admit our interest is 'me first,' and so we never face our fears.

The fact about fear is that as long as there is a 'me' — and for most of us this lasts our lifetimes — is that fear cannot be conquered, it can only be understood. It cannot be vanquished forever, it can only be seen when it occurs, and an insight into its cause will dissolve it until the next time it rears up.

Fear is one of the great problems in life. It makes us behave badly, causes hate, fights, wars. It makes us step on others to get what we want to feel safer, to steal materially and emotionally from others as if more of something could protect us. If we know what we are afraid of, and the cause of fear, it is easier to get beyond it.

The causes of fear, if you think about it, are really habit and memory, aren't they? You're fine now. You're just reading this book. What causes your fear is that pain from before could happen again, pain from the dentist, or losing a lover or a place on the team or an acceptance to college (we have memories of these pains, we have habits of fearing dentist pain and the pain of loss).

Habits and memory are just functions of thought. If you are not thinking, you are not afraid. Do not confuse intelligence, the intelligence of survival, with fear. We all jump out of the way of a Peterbilt coming at us on the highway. But psychological fear, the business of sitting around being afraid while you're really just fine isn't necessary.

But to begin with, you have to find out what you personally are afraid of. To begin with, go through the door of being ashamed, of being afraid of finding out what you're afraid of. It's time for meditation.

Sit quietly. It's hard to hear anyone else if you're twitching around and talking to yourself. Sit in your meditation place, cross-legged, in lotus position if you can, for perfect balance, back straight. Relax, as my yoga teacher says, but don't collapse.

Do some deep breathing from the belly, air in to the count of 5, hold the breath for a count of 10, breathe the air out slowly to a count of 10. This oxygenates the brain, calms the nervous system. This makes it easier for the body to sit quietly. Close or focus your eyes on a spot a few feet in front of you. The next time you breathe out, make the sound of OM or AMEN aloud in the comfortably lowest tone possible, so it resonates in your head. Hold the note for as long as you can breathe it out. This further quiets the system.

Now that you are inside your mind, drop the word *fear* in there. Find out what you are most fearful of.

Do not think, or make lists.

Just listen to yourself. We tell ourselves, as others have told us, what to think. Learn to *listen* to yourself as you would listen to a little child on your lap.

What are your deepest fears? You don't have to tell anyone else, but at least admit them to yourself so you can know yourself better.

- someone under the bed, someone hiding in the dark
- the fear of being lonely — and also of people
- death, being flung into the dark corners of the universe
- no money, job loss
- no position, being nobody, no respect, not belonging
- helplessness, being sick, in a wheelchair, blindness, being deaf
- pain, emotional, as in depression, or physical, as in beatings, torture, rape, taking too many drugs
- AIDS, pregnancy
- responsibility, school grades
- your parents will get a divorce — or they won't get a divorce
- getting fat, being short

- failing relationships with friends or lovers, that there won't be any relationships with friends or lovers

- fear of facing yourself as you are, frightened like the rest of humanity

- closed spaces, high places, fast motion, being still, wide open places

- unknown guilts, known guilts, being found out by others, being betrayed, shamed

One something we're all afraid of, and this is the silliest habit of all, is the unknown. We don't even know what is unknown, and we're afraid. Of course, what we're really afraid of is losing the known, the safety of the familiar. A good example is the fear of loneliness. We don't spend time alone because we're afraid of it, and so we never find out there's nothing to be afraid of. Death is the same thing.

You have just done a meditation. Take a deep breath and stretch your body. Know, there are no marks in meditation. Half of fear is this habit of comparison. Did I do it right? (According to whom?) Did I do it good enough? (Compared to whom?) If you learned something, you did fine. Even if all you learned was you couldn't sit still. As we said, this happens a lot to boys and men, and to many active girls. Just keep trying, until you can sit still. Even short meditations are better than no meditations at all, and the time periods will increase with interest, like every other interest, far more than with competitive comparison.

Do know that meditation, this business of waking up and paying attention is not for only an enlightened few. Anyone not in a coma can do this. And great teachers are not necessary for meditation the way they are to learn brain surgery or the art of being a good plumber. In meditation, you are your own best teacher, and sometimes the only teacher.

Know what you fear.

Knowing, it will change fear itself.

— • —

For everything there is a season, and a time for every matter...a time to be born, and a time to die;... a time to keep silence, and a time to speak....

The Preacher in Ecclesiastes 3:1,7
Old Testament, The Bible

— • —

Mere book-learning, however profound and extensive, or doing rare meritorious and apparently impossible deeds, does not enable one to obtain true enlightenment. Ask such a scholar or hero "Do you know yourself?" He will be constrained to admit his ignorance.

The guru is one who at all times abides in the profound depths of the self.

Ramana Maharshi
The Teachings

— • —

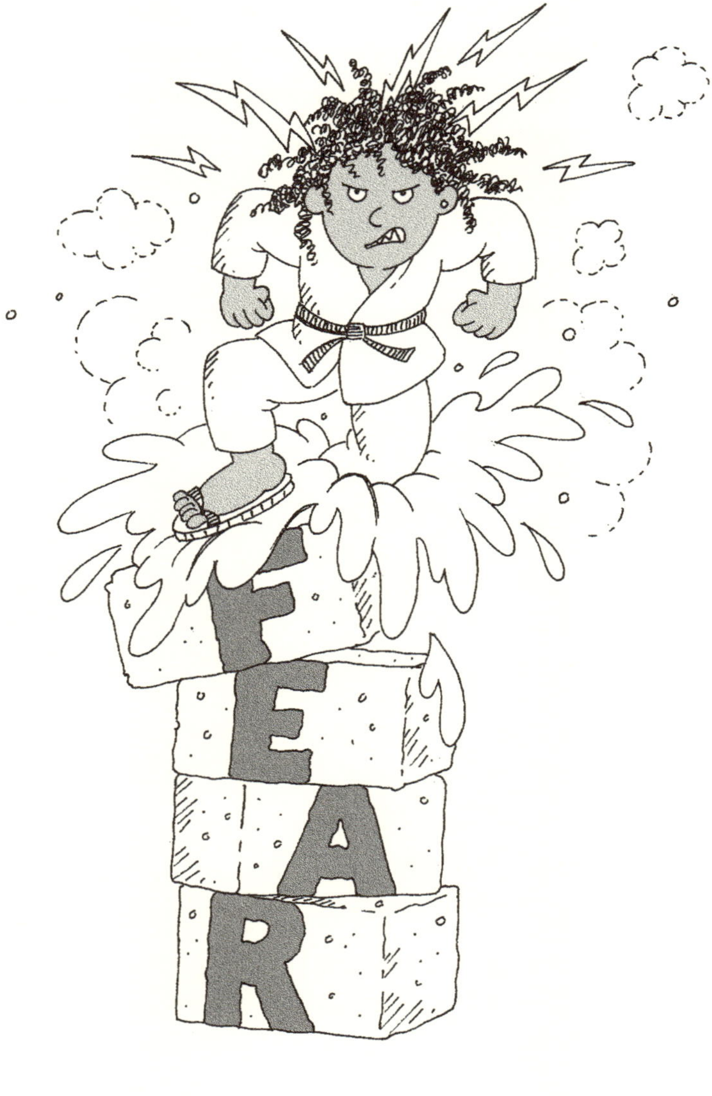
F
E
A
R

Anger

Anger based on fear probably conditions our behavior more than anything else. Angers based on our personal fears, and the fears of thousands of years of human development, are in our brains, whether we are aware of them or not. Our brains hold memories of the whole, long history of our species, whether we are aware of them or not. As a species, we are violent predators. It's a fact. You bump into me or hurt my sister, I get angry. You take something that I think is mine, my boyfriend, my bike, I get angry.

Anger is a chemical reaction, and it starts a chemical roll in us that begins with a rush and will eventually subside on its own. Now, can I *see* it, this rising of anger and *not act* on it? Because if I kick you, you'll kick me back. If I get my friends to help me, you'll get yours, and we have group, gang, national war on our hands. The trouble is, babies and other innocents get killed in the crossfire.

Can we let anger just subside instead, and then decide on the right action? Obviously, if you see a bully beating up on an old person or a child with a baseball bat, you simply take the bat away. The same way as if you see a fire, you don't stand around debating, you put it out. But the ordinary daily angers based on the fears we have, of being disrespected, taken from, ignored, can we behave differently?

Once you see that anger is a reaction to being hurt, notice what we've been conditioned to do about it. Hurt others. Or hurt ourselves. With a knife or our mouths. Or run, use escapes. Get sick. Babble out blame in an endless verbal rage. Puncture our own skin. Puncture somebody else's.

People talk about righteous anger. Is there really such a thing? People talk of crimes of passion, killing from so-called love, so-called honor. Has love got anything to do with possession, dependency, jealousy? Or is all that stuff just self warmed over! An excuse to vent angers built up over generations, over traditions, over the years of personal living.

The trouble with anger that goes unexamined is that thought turns it into resentment and it burns ourselves and others. Anger, like acid, corrodes the cup that holds it, and it doesn't matter if you're angry just at one person or everyone. Being furious may feel better than being hurt, for a while. Especially because being hurt carries the double whammy in some people of shame, of damaged pride. Someone takes my girlfriend or steals my tires, hurts my pride, makes me feel ashamed, raped. So I have to deal with the shame as well as the hurt, and together they *make me furious.*

What to do about it?

You know now; first do your sitting. Only with anger, I find in order to sit even remotely quietly, I have to do stretches first.

STRETCH EXERCISES

Stretch up.

1. Stand, feet together, back straight, hands at sides.

2. Begin deep inhalation (abdomen expands), at same time raise arms out at sides and bring overhead, palms together, raise up on heels and s-t-r-e-t-c-h up toward the ceiling, feeling your ribs lift up out of your pelvis — hold for slow 10 count.

3. Slowly back to starting point, exhaling.

4. Inhale and roll down, exhaling, lower chin to chest, slowly continue to roll down, feeling your spine's vertebrae bend over one at a time until face is as near knees as possible, stretching backs of legs. Hang for ten.

5. Spread legs wider than hips, hang for 10 more, head, shoulders, arms loose.

6. Close legs, feet together, inhale and roll up slowly.

94 • *Pay Attention To Your Brain Or It Will Kill You*

1

2

3

Anger • 95

4

5

6

Now sit in your comfortable silence position, do a few breaths, a few OM's or AMEN's, and drop the word anger into your brain. What makes you angry?

- betrayal, loss of friendship, of love, of approval
- theft, of a precious object, money, a friend
- loss of position, on the team, in the family, in your group, in class
- physical pain, helplessness, cruelty to others, to animals, to children
- feeling or being told you are inferior by family, friends, society (happens often to people who feel different or who are made to feel different, whether they are women in a society that values men, white in a place that values people of color, Hindus among Moslems, gay people among straight, blonds in China, short people on a basketball team)
- failure, success and its responsibilities, being pushed around, or being given authority

Once you know what angers you, wait for the rush to subside, then decide to do something effective about your rage instead of just catching on fire and burning yourself and everyone you run into in your flames.

The right means is action which is not the outcome of hate, envy, authority, ambition, fear...The end is the means... When you perceive for yourself that violence only leads to greater harm, is it difficult to drop violence?
  J. Krishnamurti
  Commentaries on Living
  Third Series

We seek the freedom of free men, and the construction of a world where Martin Luther King could have lived and preached non-violence.
  Nikki Giovanni
  The Funeral of Martin
  Luther King, Jr.

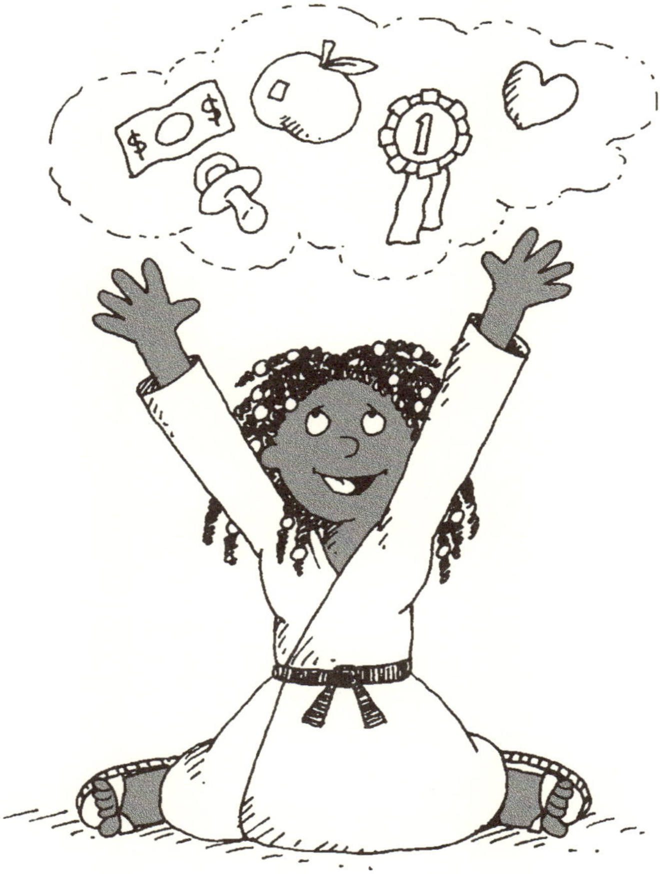

Desire And Longing

Desire, longing for something, someplace, someone, is a big problem for most of us. Desire can be sexual, it can be for power, money, position, security, comfort, to be loved, for permanent life, for immortality in the next life, for fame in this one.

Unfortunately, we've been told by too many religions and in too many societies that desire, sexual or otherwise, is wrong.

This is silly. Without desire, you're a dead person.

The problem with desire is when it gets out of hand, out of control, or in your way so it interferes with someone else's life, or your own life or leaves you strung out with depression. What do you do about it? What is desire?

Desire comes from your senses with thought added, like salt. You see a shirt you like. Nice shirt, you say. Then you *think*. It would look nice on me. I want it. I desire it. Or you see a boy or girl you want. You think, nice boy, nice girl. He, she, would look nice on me. You see a famous rock star. Fame is nice, you think. It would be nice for me, all that applause, love, attention.

Has it occurred to you that just because you want something, it doesn't truly mean you have to have it? You could see it, admire it, leave it where you found it. It's longing for everything you like that causes the problem, not the liking. It's no sin, no problem, just to admire. We have a habit of experiencing something terrific, a perfect night at a club with great music and dancing, or a perfect day at the beach skating or surfboarding, or even a moment of uninvited joy — and we think, I must have that again, I must have more. Of course, what you get the next time is just mechanical pleasure. Joy is a gift. It can't be repeated by will, as you know if you've ever tried to repeat a perfect moment.

Mostly, it's misery that causes all this wanting pleasure, isn't it? Having work to do you hate, not having a job at all, living mechanically, hardly living at all.

An overload of a particular desire just says the rest of your life is emptier than it ought to be, that your life lacks creativity, enthusiasm, joy.

So when you feel you are going crazy because you want something or someone too much, examine the rest of your life and find a way to live it better. If your own life feels good, you won't need to fix it with something or somebody else. To exercise all the muscles, for running, dancing, singing, working, brings good feelings. Not to use yourself up entirely brings depression, longing. Don't take anyone's word for any of this. Experiment with all of this yourself.

Try these practices.

SALUTE TO THE SUN

Do your sitting while focussing on a candle.

Place a lighted candle 3 feet in front of you. Sit in your meditation posture. Gaze at the flame for 2 minutes. Close your eyes and press your palms gently against your closed lids. You will see the image of the flame. Concentrate, don't wander from the image for a minute or so. Rest in your mediation posture quietly and follow your thoughts for 5 minutes, dropping the words desire and longing into your silence.

Discover what you want. Know your self's desires. Perhaps you can work for them, if they are appropriate, instead of just longing for what you want. And don't just settle for one desire, for one small corner of life: enjoy the whole, glorious, spectacular show.

— • —

That thou mayest have pleasure in everything, seek pleasure in nothing...That thou mayest possess all things, seek to possess nothing...That thou mayest be everything, seek to be nothing.

St. John of the Cross
The Ascent of Mount Carmel

— • —

These desires — for the sex relation, for material and emotional security, and for companionship — are perfectly necessary and right, and surely God-given. Self run riot is the problem.

Bill Wilson
Founder of Alcoholics Anonymous
Twelve Steps and Twelve Traditions

— • —

Desire And Longing • 103

It isn't desire that is the problem. It's what you do about desire. Needs are natural. Desire is natural. To satisfy a desire for a walk in the country, a new shirt or whatever, for food, for physical, mental, social satisfaction — all perfectly natural. Why do we make a problem of desire? Just don't hurt yourself or anyone else, or the environment, to satisfy your desires — and enjoy them.

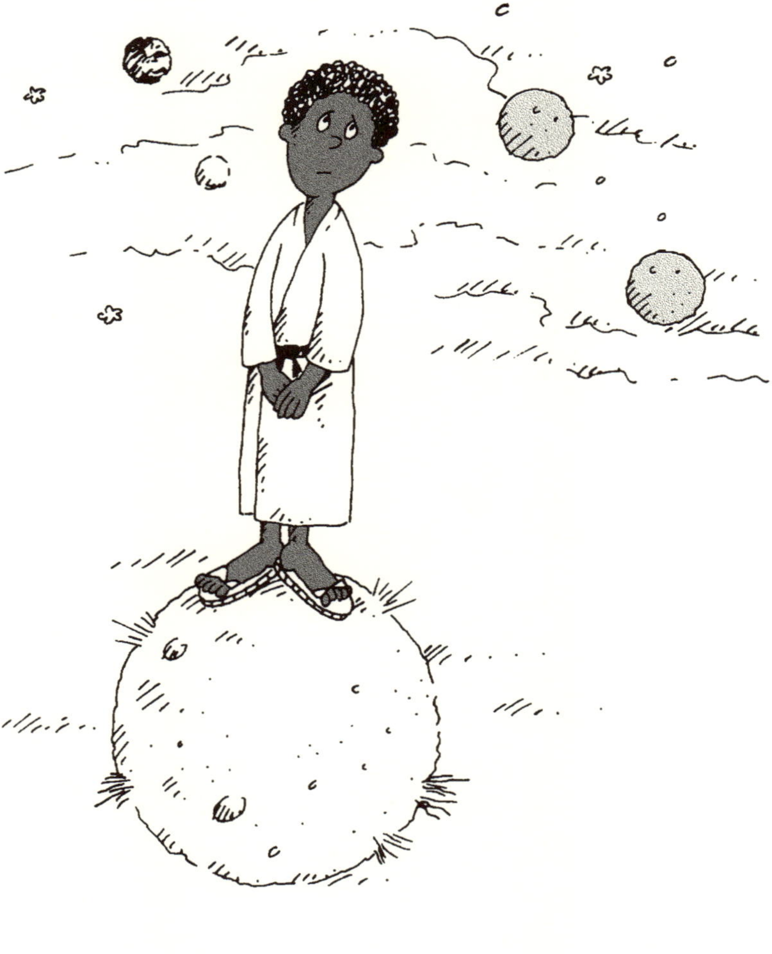

Relationship And Isolation

Why, with nearly 6 billion people in the world, do most of us feel lonely? You know that sensation, of there being nothing under you — a yawning, gaping hole where there should be firm ground. Even among friends, or family, where there ought to be close warmth and connection, there is the sudden awareness of being alone, out of touch and tune, a solitary figure at the rim of the universe.

Why is it relationship is such a struggle instead of as natural as sunlight?

After all, all life is relationship. There's a relationship, not only between people, but between you and the air you breathe, between you and the table you lean on. With these, there isn't much of a problem.

Why do we have so many problems with each other?

Is it because, out of fear and confusion, we have formed so many bad habits and one of those habits is that we *use* instead of love one another?

Teens can be the loneliest of years. There's the problem that you don't really belong in your parents' home any more, but you're not yet ready to make your own. The feeling is, if you could at least just have someone of your own to love and to love you, someone who belonged to you, someone to keep you strong, it would be like having your own private country and you'd be safe. There you'd be, the two of you against the world, Adam and Eve starting your own world.

The trouble is, it doesn't work. In a world built only for two, you end by eating each other alive.

Mating is natural. Life wants life, to reproduce itself. But in our fear of loneliness, our confusion about why humans are even here facing the vast dark unknown of the universe, we expect, we hope for more from the intimate relationship with one other person than it can possibly provide. This is just another of our bad habits based on fear that observation can correct.

Part of the problem with human relationships is words and images. Instead of seeing another person directly, if we suddenly hang the word and the image of boyfriend/girlfriend, wife/husband, parent/child on someone, we suddenly have ideas and expectations of how the other person is supposed to behave. Have you noticed this? Even your behavior changes. A once loving parent and child behave like royalty and rebel. A once independent girl acts as if her spine turned into noodles; a once nice guy acts like godzilla. You stop acting like two regular people and turn into a bad movie.

Human relationship can be a very good mirror in which to see yourself. You can see yourself, in the way you relate to your friends and family, your lover, your work, your sports, your own angers and insecurities, your own neediness, competitive rages, your own moments of generosity and kindness, all the things you are. Have a look.

But also go somewhere and look at your relationship to the clouds, the trees, nature. The truth of the sky and trees, marshes and meadows, city parks full of millions of beings living their lives in the here and now — all this truth of life just living itself knocks against our heads and what do we say? "Leave me alone, I'm searching for the truth" and it all moves back and away. Our brains are so busy telling us what we like and what we don't like, we're so full of ideas and opinions (read, hot air) about everything, we miss our whole relationship to everything around us, and the fact that our atoms are part of all the other atoms in the grass, and our *isolation and loneliness are only an attitude after all.*

Relationship And Isolation • 109

Deepen the ocean of your consciousness with attention to what is true. As the great writer Somerset Maugham once said, and I'm quoting very roughly, "Before you get smart, you think you're a separate drop of water in the ocean. When you get smarter, you decide to join the rest of the drops of water in the ocean. Real intelligence is to see you've been part of the ocean all along."

What is love then, you ask?

Easier to see, as you look at yourself and understand yourself in relationship, what love is *not*.

- love is not clutching at another person for dear life to keep *you* alive (think of life-saving techniques in the water: a stranglehold around the rescuer's neck and you both go underwater)

- love is not dependency — obviously it's good to hold hands and keep each other company and comfort one another when life hurts, but fight to see who can sit on the other's lap first, and you both fall on the floor

- love is not using another for strength— only vampires suck another's blood

- love isn't possession, jealousy, control (this statement is not an excuse for promiscuity, or running around and playing with everybody's lives)

- love is not a sentiment, not just a mood for who or what it's in the mood for

Love loves. Not just for a return on investment. Actually, love is a state of being without an actual object. It's a state of communion, connection, affection, with no goals, no ulterior motives. No self. Where the self is, love is not.

Before sitting to face the embarrassment of how you are in relationship (at least for most of us, facing how angry, needy, and manipulating we are in relationship to other people is embarrassing), try a relaxation exercise.

1. Lie flat on floor or bed.

2. Tense every muscle group one after the other, beginning with toes, feet, legs, buttocks, and up the back to shoulders, arms, fists, then up the neck to the face, squeezing the face together like a prune.

3. Take a deep breath. Let go suddenly, all the muscles and the breath.

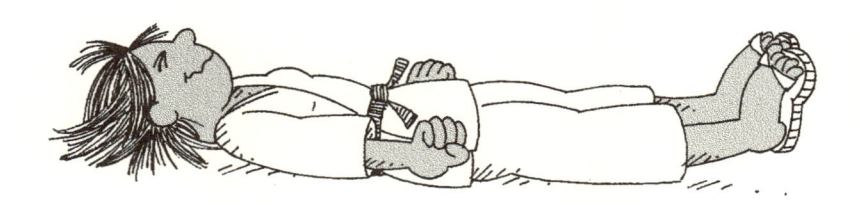

4. Now relax all the muscles in the same order. With attention, relax every muscle group one after the other, toes, feet, legs, buttocks, back, arms, hands, neck, head, face.

5. Do 5 deep meditation breaths, slowly filling the belly for 5, push air up into lungs, hold for 10, breathe slowly out for 10.

Now do your sitting. Into your silence drop the words loneliness, then relationship. What do you learn about yourself?

— • —

There is a common need to escape, and mutually we use each other. This usage is called love. You do not like what you are, and so you run away from yourself.
J. Krishnamurti
Total Freedom

— • —

Avoid becoming a mirror image of those men who value power above life, and control over love.
Maya Angelou
Wouldn't Take Nothing
For My Journey Now

— • —

I AM:
BAD
GOOD
UGLY
OKAY
A LOSER
STUPID
SMARTER THAN MY FRIEND TONY
PRETTY
STRONG
A WIMP
TOO FAT
TOO THIN
ETC ETC ETC ETC ETC ETC ETC

Self-Awareness, Self-Knowledge, The Keys To Freedom And Power

I don't know about you, but I like to take my shower by myself.

Unfortunately, there are still times when the tub is so crammed with people in my head all talking and shouting, I want to run screaming for the hills. You know the feeling? All you're doing is washing your chest, and your brain starts imaging your mother, your father, your teachers, your friends all having opinions about you.

Then, to make it even noisier, you start answering back. You supply judge, jury, prosecutor, defense lawyer, and yourself as defendant, all yelling at you and over you until the surrounding sound is deafening. No opinion is left unchallenged. No conclusion is ever reached. You're good. You're bad. You're ugly. I'm not. You're good-looking. You're fat. You're strong. You're a wimp. I'm powerful, my friends hang with me, I've got four team letters, I'm editor of the paper, I solved the structure in biochemistry. Yeah, but you lost a race last week, you've got pimples on your back, maybe your friends don't really like you, and anyway, your father says….

This is **not** self-awareness. This is **not** self-knowledge. **This** is just craziness.

To be aware, is to observe what you're doing, thinking, feeling, without judging, without calling yourself more names. And if there's name-calling, just observe that without agreeing with the names.

Yesterday, I yelled at my friend about being such a wuss she let her boyfriend drink too much and then make love to her. The whole time in my shower, I was carrying on an argument about whether I was right to yell at her for her own sake, whether I was wrong to yell, whether I was in a bad mood, jealous that she had a boyfriend, scared about all the drinking and sex, on and on and on. Wrong way to stop the noise.

I climbed out of the shower, got warm and dry, sat quietly in my silent-sitting place, did a few OM's, some deep breathing. My brain shut up long enough for me to have a perfectly clear observation with no name-calling.

There was nothing wrong and everything right about caring enough about my friend to tell her the truth. There was everything wrong and nothing right about yelling at her at the top of my lungs about it just because I was scared and depressed over being female and a teenager. Further, was there a way of expressing all this without the usual, human mechanical programming of turning fear into anger?

What we are asking is, can there be an observation of the self without the "I" coming into it — because it is the "I" that contains the echo chamber for all those remembered voices. And all those voices, all those perceptions *are* the "I" now, *are* the "you."

It is *so* hard to get this.

— • —

"Thou art that." The Sanscrit doctrine...asserts that everything you think you are and everything you think you perceive are undivided. To realize fully this lack of division is to become enlightened...Logic presumes a separation of subject from object, therefore logic is not final wisdom. The illusion of separation of subject from object is best removed by the elimination of physical activity, mental activity and emotional activity.

Robert M. Persig
Zen and the Art of
Motorcycle Maintenance

— • —

In quantum physics, it was discovered that the *observer* affected the *observed* and changed what it was observing. Meditation, observation, **can** change your life.

Our brains are about three pounds of cells that coordinate our senses. There's no central "I" anyway, as we see, but there *are* receptor cells to receive the underlying intelligence of the universe (that some call god or conscience), a kind of cable TV hookup to the cosmos. These receptors can know the truth about any situation because right action, right attitude isn't based on choice, like, mood: it's based on understanding what's right for any given situation. There is, for instance, never a right choice for cruelty, for prejudice, for killing, for ruining the environment. These are mental illnesses, illnesses of individuals and groups, caused by a breakdown of the receptors that link your life to the living universe. Obviously right action and attitude is based on what's good for everyone, not just you and yours. And while you may need adults to teach you how to build a wagon so every generation doesn't have to waste time reinventing the wheel, there's little point in asking most of the previous generation how to live life: after all, we're still running the world wrong. Some scientists think the human species has even regressed, as our wars are still killing little children, we are still ruining the planet instead of protecting the very environment we need for life to continue. Meditate and connect, ask yourselves how to act rightly on your own.

A scientific note here about so-called progress from the great science writer, Stephen Jay Gould. In his book *Full House*, he says that there is no evolution to a human pinnacle of life. He says that there is just variation in the great bush of life, lots of changing varieties of lots of species. Humans are only one variety of life, complicated but not necessarily better. After all, he says, 80 percent of life is bacteria, not us. What we have is "consciousness — the factor that permits us, rather than any other species, to ruminate... but how can this invention be viewed as the distillation of life's primary thrust or direction when 80 percent [of life] enjoys such evolutionary success and displays no trend to...

complexity — and when our own neural elaboration may just as well end up destroying us." His point is that humans have arrogantly — and clearly mistakenly — appointed themselves top dogs.

Awareness, then, is to understand that this *selfness* we've all been educated to believe is so precious, is, in point of fact, not only unreal, but the enemy. In protecting the self — in our deep confusion over what we are doing in this vast universe, why we are here, where we are going — we form habits of thinking that hurt us and hide the truth. Seeing the truth of all this, on the other hand, might give us eternity.

— • —

To accept naturally without self-importance:
If you never assume importance
You never lose it."

Lao Tzu
The Way of Life

— • —

The meek shall inherit the earth.

Jesus of Nazareth
The Bible

— • —

Meek, incidentally, has nothing to do with grovelling: it means those without self-importance.

What they're all saying, the wise ones, and it's something you don't have to accept but can discover for yourself, is — behave, and you've got power, and freedom.

P.S.   You'll be wondering by now perhaps why more people don't wander these paths, these inner lands of the mind. It's because it's hard country. Few people travel here. There's no material profit, no promotion. But for those who make the journey, the beauty, the joy, is worth the difficulty. Freedom is the reward, from the crushing pain of the life of the self. This land has a vast sweep, no certainty. Those who go there have no choice.

And, it must be said again, everyone has what it takes to travel here. Everyone, every brain, has the capacity. Some say that only certain physicists (specialists in the natural sciences), and metaphysicists (people who understand the relationship of our nature to the universe) can access whatever capacities lead to understanding — people like Galileo and Einstein, Christ, the Buddha, Krishnamurti.

What Galileo and Einstein, Christ, the Buddha, Krishnamurti said, though, is that we can all do it, that every brain has this ability. David Bohm added, that since we only use about 15 percent of our brain cells that we know about, imagine what all those unconditioned cells could do. What it takes, they all said, is to be able to listen, and you can only listen in silence.

Sit.

Find silence.

Success And Failure

Comparison is the psychological killer. And it makes you nervous whether the comparison is positive or negative.

You may not be as tall as your brother, but you're smarter.

Where does that leave you? Feeling worthless because you're short in a tall society, and causing your brother to hate you all your life because he's been told he's stupid and you're the smart one.

You're as clever as your Aunt Gertrude (you know, the one who won the Nobel Prize in physics.)

What choices does that give you? If you don't do physics and try for the Nobel Prize, you're thrown the family heritage back in their faces and what's more, you're an underachiever, and an ingrate. If you do grit your teeth and go for it, and you don't win any prizes, you're a failure.

You're as pretty as a movie star.

Do you have to prove this by being a movie star, and if you don't make it, that may mean you're not really pretty after all, they were lying to you, and if they were lying about that, what else were they lying about to cover up the fact that you're probably absolutely worthless.

My son, he's a better football player than I ever was, a real candidate for the Heisman Trophy.

Crushing. Your life is laid out for you — a long, long competition, to be better than your dad down through the decades of your years.

Can we do without this? Why must we compete and compare?

Unfortunately, it may be because millions of years ago, all life had to compete to survive and the food went to the fastest, the strongest, the cleverest. If a zebra didn't keep up with the herd, not only didn't she get any grass to eat, or what was left to drink at the drying water hole, she might well become the lion's lunch. Now, however, in this country at least, we can just go to the supermarket, most of us. It isn't necessary to be a speed freak or a competitive killer just to stay alive.

Because that's what comparison does, it turns us into killers. Comparison teaches children very young that it is nec-

Success And Failure • 125

essary to compete: for approval; for a place in the sun; for love and favor, if not for actual food.

What it teaches us, even more deeply, is *that we are never all right the way we are.* Watch a friend's face sometime when you compare your friend to someone else. Watch your own inner feelings, when you are compared. Even if the comparison is cheerful for a moment, the inner dialogue begins: *am I really better? do I have to try harder to stay better? could that opinion change with the wind?*

All comparison creates is anxiousness, or even outright anger at the constant presence of someone else's yardstick. It creates inner demons that last a lifetime.

Grades at school, prizes for best-competitor-of-the-day, all this creates mayhem in the hearts of the young and not-so-young. It creates tension, ambition, greed, lust for the prize, and an agreeable willingness to do anything to win that may or may not stop short of murder, at least in the heart.

It is perfectly possible to teach children, and ourselves to do our best, to stretch ourselves to the fullest capacity, to develop all our skills, without even mentioning the words **success and failure.** *People don't have to spend their years wondering what happens to them if they're not a success.*

In this sitting, today, discover as you watch the flow of the outer world into your inner world and the effects it has on you, what comparisons have driven you to — either into shriveling up in a corner and not trying, or into the kind of fierce competition for glory that leaves you with bitten nails, an anorexic or pumped-up body, mood swings that range from suicidal depression at failure or the thought of it to the giddy highs of a win that drive you on to the next win like an addict to the next hit.

The point here is that you can be and do all you like. Competition is doing something to beat others: doing your best is stretching yourself to your fullest capacity.

Try these stretches to illustrate the point physically.

- *Side bend.*
- *Back bend.*
- *Forward bend.*

Practice these stretches, without looking in the mirror to see how you're doing, to compare with anyone else. Just stretch and feel good.

— • —

...the human psyche finds comfort in alternately embracing... the two poles of the false self: namely, the grandiose self developed in compliance with the parents' demands and in constant need of admiration, and the empty self, alone and impoverished, alienated and insecure, aware only of the love that was never given.

Mark Epstein, M.D.
Thoughts Without A Thinker

— • —

When you see this, you can ignore both faces of the false self and just enjoy your life, doing your best some days, taking a nap some days.

Loneliness, Depression, And Suffering

Loneliness is the painful discovery of our emptiness, the feeling of being completely cut off from everyone, everything. Because we haven't been told that the mind is normally empty, that there is no self, the discovery of our own emptiness fills us with fear. Even people with a strong idea of self know the self is gappy, there are fearful moments when it disappears. This emptiness and the fear cause depression and lead us to all the escapes that hurt us even further.

What we never do is stop to look at this emptiness, to see it for what it is. Instead of seeing the empty mind, those gaps between thoughts, as a beautiful, quiet, empty pool for beauty to pour into us, it scares us. Nobody ever talks about it as something wonderful. So we fill it with busyness. We just run from it as fast as our little legs can carry us. We run straight for dependencies to fill the void, other people, food, drugs, things — and when these fail us, we pour ourselves into work, sports, television, the computer, music, movies, service.

It's so weird. The very thing loneliness wants is for something real and alive to come in. But how can anything be poured into a full cup? Have you ever taken a walk or sat in a puddle of sunlight when you had the delicious feeling of being alone, with the whole loveliness of life pouring into you? Then you know being alone feels whole, in connection with everything. It isn't the same thing as loneliness.

Loneliness is a terrible enemy. Loneliness can create depressions, sufferings so bad that people drink themselves into alcoholism, drug themselves into addiction, cut themselves, starve their bodies into anorexia and their souls into isolation or criminal rage. Many teenage girls go inward into suicidal isolation. In teenage boys, depression often takes the form of agitation and anger and antisocial behavior.

The greatest fear about loneliness is that it will never end. To see that we can be alone, empty without fear, is to see the truth. Once you see it, you'll never panic again. Lonely feelings will simply turn into the pleasure of being alone. People will come into your life and go. Things will come into your life and go. The tides come in. The tides go out, and you're fine. They'll come in again. They always do.

When the mind understands the utter uselessness of trying to fill its own emptiness with dependencies, whether this is through knowledge, belief, people, or drugs, when it truly discovers it can't run away from its own emptiness, it makes friends with that emptiness, and the fear goes away.

When I was in India, I asked my teenage class to describe loneliness. Their words were identical to my teenage class on the shoreline of Connecticut, and the teenagers I taught in Harlem, New York. And there are a billion people living together in India, in large close families, with no language for privacy, never mind an opportunity for any.

I asked them to join me in a group silence. I dropped the word loneliness into our silence. Twenty-three quiet teenage Indian girls in their saris, and twenty teenage boys in white kurta-pajama were dutifully quiet. We did several deep breaths. The sounds of babbler birds and the whisper of the breeze through the leaves of the pipal tree stirred the dust and heat of India's afternoon. A sudden shriek of monkeys ended our silence.

"With respect for your mental privacy, it would be helpful to all of us if anyone wanted to begin the dialogue on what you discovered about loneliness. What does loneliness feel like to you?" I asked.

An Indian boy answered:

"Loneliness is the feeling of being completely cut off from everyone — there is nothing you can depend on."

A girl in the India class said:

"Loneliness is like dying all the time. You can't touch anything or anyone. You're in the dark, by yourself, you can't communicate. Everything, everyone is far away."

A boy in the Connecticut class, wrote:

"What loneliness feels like is a deep, sunless pain, as if you had been flung into a dark corner of the universe, or beneath the depths of the sea. No one can reach you."

A girl from Harlem said:

"Even when you get it that the self isn't real, it still feels real, and it — you — still feel lonely."

Boy and girl, Indian and American, all said the same things.

They all described the frantic search for an escape, a rope to pull them up and out of the deep well of loneliness, a boat to sail out of the empty sea to shore, any shore. Any boat.

— • —

It is a rare being who can cross the ocean of existence without a boat.

> Richard Alpert (Ram Dass)
> Journey of Awakening

— • —

Loneliness, Depression, And Suffering • 133

Teachers, friends, lovers, organizations, methods — we use all of these as boats, just something to carry us for a while until we can get our balance, our strength back, to continue our journey.

The trouble with using boats, though, is they can turn into traps and weaken you, into illusions of safety that delay your journey toward freedom from pain.

If you use a boat, just remember it's a temporary raft, not a safe haven. Don't confuse it with the real thing. Don't confuse being in love with loving; good works with goodness; a sermon about god with your own real connection to god.

Sometimes the following meditations (awarenesses, ponderings, insights) can help:

- it helps to know we're all in the same place, all people have pretty much the same feelings, so you can hold mental hands with the rest of us lonely souls

- meditation, awareness, is the awakening of intelligence that sees there is no "me" and no "you," no "we" and "they," and that only a small part of the brain involved with thought has created all this separation
- so if you dissolve "I" and "you" and separation ends, loneliness ends
- you can use a different part of your brain than thought as the dissolvent (awareness, insight, universal receptors – those receivers every brain has for the intelligence of the universe, meditation)
- sometimes you can really see that loneliness is just a habit of thought, like anger, fear, and so many other psychological aches and pains — something we have been taught to feel when we are alone, rather than something we actually even feel
- you may discover, as a lot of us have, that being on your own, being alone, is not the same as loneliness: it can be like a good run — a little hard at first, but in the end, exhilarating and freeing

And sometimes nothing helps. You have to just sit it out until it passes and you can use your intelligence to see through loneliness once more.

When I get stuck, as you can see from this book, I use writing meditation. I just write about what's going on with me until it becomes clear and goes away.

When I get too stuck in my own psychological and spiritual melodrama, I also remember the prayer of St. Francis when he went through his own emotional troubles.

— • —

Lord, make me a channel of thy peace…grant that I may seek rather to comfort than to be comforted, to understand, than to be understood, to love, than to be loved. For it is by self-forgetting than one finds.

— • —

It can help to go be nice to somebody else in the same boat. Do a 2-5 minute group silent sitting and have a dialogue after your silence about relationship, and loneliness.

Sex

Sex is natural. It is as natural to life as eating, sleeping, breathing. Why do we make such a problem of it? Is it the pleasure? The escape? The power? Is it that there is relationship to another, a moment of connection to prove we aren't alone under the sky?

Surely we must question our demands, especially the ones that turn into problems, instead of just give in to them. Otherwise, they'll drive us crazy. To understand, we have to look at the mind behind the act.

Too often, society has said that we must control sexual behavior. Parents, teachers, Western priests, and Asian holy men, have all said in different languages, put a lid on it.

We all know that doesn't work, either. Sex is normal and natural, it is very beautiful when it isn't contaminated with abuse, when it is part of love and maturity and consideration of the other person, of all possible consequences. It only becomes a problem when it's abused.

Because you have been sitting in silence, meditating, you already know there is another way of putting an end to problems: not through rules and other people's regulations, but through your own insight or understanding.

So, sit. Perhaps a few stretches or yoga exercises, martial arts forms, calisthenics, aerobics, mantras like AMEN, OM, chanting or prayers, or just some deep breaths to settle down the body and oxygenate the brain so you can sit still.

Consider. Why, when we know about unwanted pregnancies that bring children into the world that no one really wants to take care of; why, when we know the dangers of AIDS, STD's (sexually transmitted diseases); why, when we know that too much sex with too many people too early in our lives degenerates the beauty of a truly loving lifelong relationship as adults; why do we go on having too much sex with too many people, too young, too often?

Remember, in meditation, we don't judge. We consider. Consider some of the following possibilities.

- sex is an intense physical pleasure that's free of cost and instantly available without having to go to a store, locate a dealer, buy a ticket — and the pleasure is only intensified by being culturally forbidden, whether that's homosexual sex, cross-cultural/cross-color-line sex, or across-generation sex (never mind criminal sex: rape, pedophilia, incest, sadomasochism)—and when sex does cost, there's the pleasure of a business transaction

- sex is a marvelous escape from the self and its worries, pains, anxieties

- sex is a power trip over another person to get back feelings of appreciation, for being pretty or handsome, popular even for that moment, being wanted, just being stronger if you're male, sexier than the competition if you're female

- sex is momentarily the best antidote to loneliness — except for the moment when it is over and you never felt lonelier in your life, because sex without love never works for long

A good question to consider also, is why are our lives so empty that we include sex among our other addictions? Surely that's the point. Obviously, if we are living fully, living creatively, sex is only part of life and we can wait for it for the proper time, place, age. If our lives are empty, frightening, and we think we have to clutch at each other's bodies for comfort, surely it is better to put some energy into improving the quality of the rest of our lives so sex isn't the only great pleasure.

Yes, it's true sex is all around our culture; on television, in the movies, in ads for cars and undershorts, in popular music, in books and magazines. So what? Colds are all around, too. Do you have to catch them?

No one has to tell you that sex doesn't work for long as a tool for living, and that it has serious emotional and physical complications. No one has to tell you about the psychological complications, either. There is *no such thing as casual sex*. Sex opens up the most intimate vulnerabilities in our deepest emotions because sex is the most intimate arrangement of bodies. Minds and bodies *are* connected.

We live in our bodies, like it or not. What you eat affects you, what you breathe in affects you. What you hear, smell, whatever you put in your brain affects you. What you do about sex affects you, too.

If you want to be holy (Sanscrit for 'healthy' or 'wholesome'), be careful what you put in your holes.
Indian Holy Man

— • —

As always, it turns out nature isn't the problem, it's our thinking and our thoughts, and, as the great theoretical physicist David Bohm puts it, our feelings and our felts.

— • —

People pay very little attention to how they are thinking. They don't see that all these crises are due to the way we think. They say they want to solve these crises, yet they want to go on with the same way of thinking. It doesn't make sense.
David Bohm
Dialogue with Students
Oak Grove School, CA

— • —

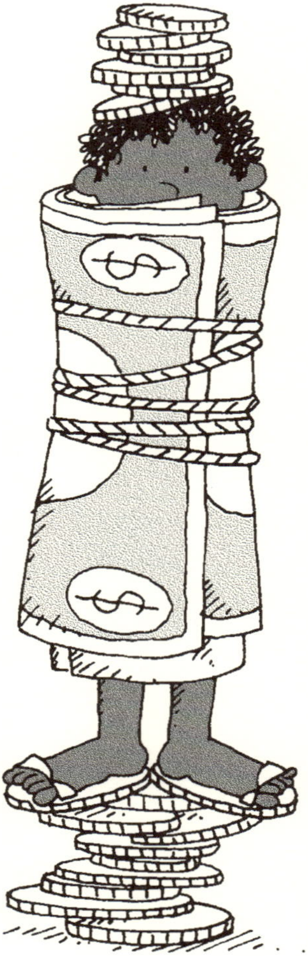

Money

Money is fine. There's nothing wrong with money. It is what it is, a simple form of trading commodity, easier to carry in your pocket if you want a dozen eggs and half a house built than a mule to trade. If you don't have enough money to feed yourself, cover your body, and put a roof over your head, then someone else has to feed you, buy you a sweater, build you a house. For the most part, people resent having to do this for anyone over the age of sixteen.

But that's all money is.

Neurotics, holier-than-thou types, and people with too much of it look down on money with contempt.

Neurotics, scared, and greedy people (these are just other words for ambition) look up to money as if it gave them status and power and great influence. (Have you noticed yet that the most powerful, influential status always comes from that rarest of all things, not money, but goodness? Whose names have lasted longer, with more star quality, than Jesus Christ, Mohammed, Buddha, Moses, Mother Mary, Mother Nature, God?)

When I traveled and taught in India, wandering around with the rest of the seekers of truth because I still hadn't discovered that the stuff was inside me, not outside, I watched and listened to people. What struck me continually was the muttering of Americans clucking over what they called India's poverty. Especially in Mother Teresa's Calcutta where so many of us worked with the Missionaries of Charity in the Mission for the Destitute Dying, they shook their heads over families living on a patch of pavement with their babies and their few pots on a bit of cloth, bathing at the street pump and sharing what little they had. They couldn't seem to see what was obvious. The families's faces shone and smiled at each other with love; the faces of the Americans were ugly with what Mother Teresa always called the poverty of loneliness, the fear that what they had might be stolen from them.

We've been talking about the brain's conditioning: in different countries, different qualities are valued and taught to the children. In China and Japan, it is duty. In France, intellect and lineage. In India, caste. In England, class. In the United States? You know. Money.

Money, Americans say, is the reward of the ambitious. Our culture has taught that without ambition, nothing is accomplished: good grades, leading to good colleges, leading to good jobs, leading to better jobs and lots of money. But is it true that without ambition, nothing is accomplished? A carpenter can build a beautiful house without ambition, because he loves his work. A machinist can become an electrical engineer because she wants to build a marvelous car, not because she wants to be president of General Motors and earn a lot of position and money. Perhaps far more can be accomplished for the love of it, whatever the work we do, than for financial reward. Look at all those tired, miserable faces in traffic jams, in malls, plugging away at work they find boring, repetitive, mechanical, for their whole lives, because they've been taught to live with ambition for more position, for more money.

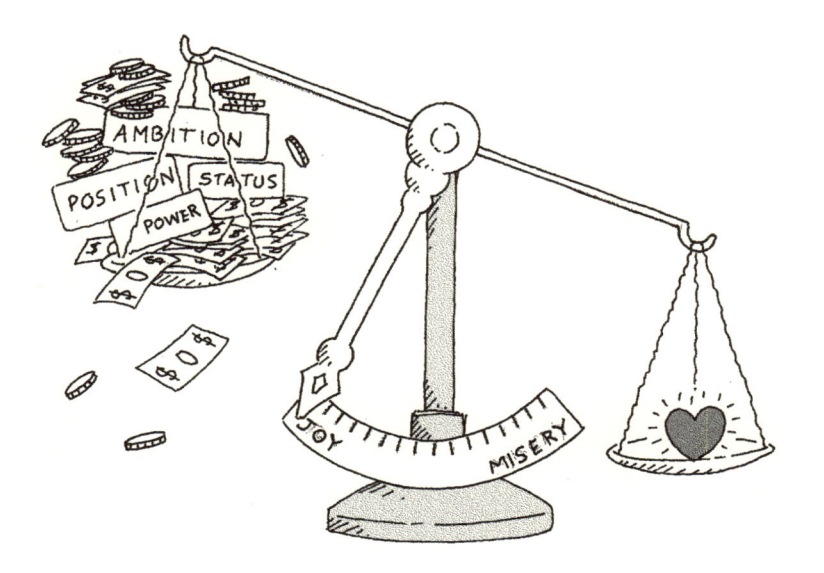

Ambition is, after all, just self-importance. And we're learning about the trap, the prison of the self and its nonsense. Can we break with tradition and the jail of safety, to live instead with the fun of doing what we like, what we enjoy, because this gives our lives joy?

This doesn't mean don't earn money. After all, as we said, nobody wants to go on forever providing you with food, clothing, shelter. But don't confuse function with position or money. After all, there's always going to be somebody who's got more position, more money, more power. After all, success is just another invention of society, another bit of programming. Do what you love to do, do it the best you can, work well, be happy.

Doubt what you've been told. Examine what you think you've been handed as the truth. Do a sitting and find out what money means to you.

— • —

Let go the things in which you are in doubt for the things in which there is no doubt.

Mohammed
The Koran

— • —

Education

There was once a teacher who announced to her class that she thought grades were as dangerous to people's minds as falling in front of a truck was to their bodies. She announced that she had no intention of grading her writing class for the short novels she intended teaching them to write that year, that she would simply pass or fail them depending on whether they completed their books.

She could hardly believe the dismay on her students' faces. She had seen the excitement on their faces the day before when she said that anyone could write a book, that not everyone was going to live the life of a writer, but that whatever they did, they might want to write a book about their field of activity, about their lives — and she was going to teach them the technique. They had been enthusiastic about writing books. Now, suddenly, they were negative. What was that about?

What was wrong with our educational system that our students only want to learn in exchange for grades? What would make it different so our students actually want an education? After all, what the survival of our species is based on and one of the factors that distinguishes the human brain, is curiosity: about the stars, about ourselves, about the purpose of life, our place in the whole spectrum of life in the universe, about nature, about the nature of life itself.

At what point, and why, did this natural interest in learning warp out of shape and turn into fear in the form of a scramble for success that in school takes the form of good grades?

Examine your own responses to the reactions of this class. What are your own purposes in education? See if you agree with your conditioning. See if you want to make some changes in the attitudes you've been handed down. You may want to keep some, change some.

"My family expects good grades."

"I want my father to be proud of me."

"I can only get a good job or get into a good college if I have good grades."

"I feel like such a loser if I don't get A's."

"What's the point in doing the work if you don't get grades?"

"I'm scared to go home if I don't get good grades."

Many students expose the hypocrisy of our educational system. We have taught them to keep an eye on the prize, on the piece of paper at the end, the one without which we won't give them a degree, without which we won't give them a higher education, a decent job, a place in society. Under this system, without grades, a lot of students would probably not do the work, flunk themselves out, and go get jobs they don't like.

Of course, this might be a good thing. They might end by hating the boring, repetitive jobs, come back and really want to learn something meaningful, apply themselves to engineering to replace factory work, or hotel management to replace fast food service or developmental psychology to augment domesticity. They might discover they want to learn carpentry, masonry, engine repair, how to run a small business. They would come back to school motivated to learn so their lives might be stimulating instead of boring. And they would insist on an excellent education because they were paying for it, because they knew the penalty of living dumb, repetitive days, day after boring day.

As young as preschool age, society begins to teach its children to compete, to envy, to battle each other for preference or for the best grades. We use the excuse that we have to teach them skills to make a living. Of course we all have to learn those skills in math and science, writing, and so forth, so we can make a living. But if we don't also teach skills in living itself, we don't end up with a cooperative, productive society, we end up with combat. The same children who hit each other over the head with shovels in the sandbox, the same children who competed for grades, the same children who were not taught the beauty of a flower but only its name, will turn into adults who trample life instead of loving its bloom.

And speaking of bloom, that's what education is for. To help a young person bloom. To help students find out what interests them, not us, to learn. Either to make a living at, or if that isn't possible, to enjoy in their spare time.

The root meaning of *educare* (Latin) is to lead or draw out, not stuff in.

— • —

In our stress and struggle with our children to get their skills accomplished, there is the opportunity for us to examine ourselves as parents, as people, as grown up children. After all, we want more for our children than for them to join the rat race of competitive career chasing and ladder climbing. There appears to be more conflict in the world, in our communities, and our schools than ever before. What is it our children are really learning? What are they observing and attending in our lessons and the classes at school?... We, as parents and early childhood care-givers are responsible for examining in ourselves what we think we are teaching and what our children are learning.

Hannah Carlson, M.Ed., C.R.C.
Director, Discovery Days Day Care Center

— • —

The real issue is the quality of our mind: not its knowledge but the depth of the mind that meets knowledge. Mind is infinite, is the nature of the universe which has its own order, has its own immense energy. It is everlastingly free. The brain, as it is now, is the slave of knowledge...Education then is freedom from conditioning, from its vast accumulated knowledge as tradition. This does not deny the academic disciplines which have their own proper place in life.

J. Krishnamurti, October 1, 1982
Letters to the Schools, Volume 2

— • —

Change your thinking now. If you don't change your thinking now, tomorrow will be the same as today.

Ray Fisher
Unpublished Dialogues

Obviously, you can't single-handedly change a national system tomorrow afternoon. What you can do is examine your own motives in seeking an education, pay attention to your own attitudes, and lay new paths in your own brain with different behavior, different thinking. Do remember, everything, every thought, every attitude affects not only the chemistry in your own brain, but everything else, whether it's immediately visible or not. How often have you heard something that made no sense to you at the time but you understood days, weeks, years later on? So, plant seeds.

Rebellion is a waste of energy. True revolution is an inside job. But if you speak up, act differently in school or at the dinner table at home, if you change your own attitudes about education and what it means, you can change other attitudes wherever you go.

As always, begin with yourself. If you just see the truth of something, it will change your life, because you won't be able to buy the lie anymore. Then, perhaps, talk to a receptive teacher, other students. Don't worry if you sound different. As we have pointed out, a million people can be absolutely wrong.

Love: Not Self, Dependency, Thought, Or Image

The neurotic disturbance in our culture, that compound of sex, biology, loneliness, the need for security, the passion for possession and power, dependency in a relabeled need for parenting, and addiction with its desperate highs and equally desperate withdrawals, an inability to stand on one's own two feet, the emptiness that requires drama and a part in the movie script or at least a few hours attention — all of this is what we have called 'being in love.'

Those with an extra scrap of intelligence see through it at least enough to suspect they are simply rationalizing chemistry, and distinguish between speaking English (or Chinese, French, Swahili, Cherokee), and luvspeak. Most popular songs and country music lyrics describe being in love in the words generally used to describe an anxiety attack when you can't get your breath.

How can we promise to 'love forever?' You do or you don't. You will or you won't. It's one day at a time like everything else. Don't forget the marriage vows were invented when people didn't live much past 28 or 30 years old — not too long a forever for the average romance.

And we say not only, I love you. We say, I love that movie. I love pizza. I love god. I love my mom. I love my country. I love football. What *are* we going on about?

When we say, aren't I supposed to love my race, my nation, my group, what are we talking about? We are all one, we are human beings, not labels. We have artificially created nations and races in our search for power and security, through greed, ill-will, and general idiocy out of which we arrange for prejudice, war, drive-by shootings, slavery and holocausts. What's so hot about loving and honoring all this?

And when we talk about a love relationship, what we really mean is the security of ownership.

Ask most people what they mean by 'love.' My friend the philosopher Ray Fisher once asked me that question some years ago, and the way I answered, he said, made me sound as if the other person was a country I was colonizing. Ask your friends, or just listen to them. What you'll hear is, "he's mine," "she's my girl," "that's my wife." Think how often, during a love affair, you've heard or thought, "you belong to me."

Clearly, love is not ownership, jealousy, possessiveness, pride, security, dependency, a drug-of-choice, a hiding-place from the confusion and loneliness of life. It isn't just a word to be used about parents, children, mates, friends, pets, rituals, because of all the gratification they give you. Love isn't the activity of do-gooders and politicians, ambition or acquisition.

— • —

Love is not to be divided as the love of God and the love of man, nor is it to be measured as the love of one and of the many. Love gives itself abundantly as a flower gives its perfume; but we are always measuring love in our relationship and thereby destroying it…

In the total development of the human being through right education, the quality of love must be nourished and sustained from the very beginning…this quality of love, which is humility, gentleness, consideration, patience, and courtesy. Modesty and courtesy are innate in the person of right education…considerate to all, including the animals and plants, and this is reflected in behavior and manner of talking….[It] frees the mind from its absorption in its ambition, greed.

J. Krishnamurti
Total Freedom

— • —

— • —

Love is the ultimate and real need in every human being.
Erich Fromm
The Art of Loving

— • —

None of this means don't be in love with your sweetheart, don't love the rolling hills and the winter snows of the country you live in, the generosity of your parents and teachers, the sport or music you love to play. It simply means don't use them for your own gratification (dependency and need and control are taking, love only gives), and don't exclude everything and everyone else from that affection. It means no images for someone to have to live up to, no rules, regulations. (This does not mean we are free to be promiscuous or inconsiderate; it means don't keep a suit of shining armor or a size four princess dress/bikini in your garage someone has to fit into.) These images we make up prevent connection with anyone psychologically. We relate to pictures our thought makes up of people, and we live in isolated disappointment, bitterness, and loneliness when people don't match the movie we have made up about them.

Love is a state of being, not attached only to one person or object. Where the self is, with its uproar of thoughts, needs, dependencies, expectations, and images, love is *not*.

Love: Not Self, Dependency, Thought, Or Image • 159

Certainly, you have suspected all this. Certainly, you have heard the words, I love you, and known perfectly well you were smelling mendacity in the air, betrayal, a bargain-hunter.

But never mind other people; there isn't much you can do about them. Be mindful of yourself.

Sit for a while. Try something called vipasana. It's a focus on the breath. A courageous woman prison official, Kiran Bedi, arranged for thousands of prisoners in India to learn vipasana. Teachers were asked to help these violent and sad and lonely human beings go on an inward journey, to help them understand their own ways, their own minds. It's an interesting journey. They sat still, without speaking, focussing on the breath so the mind didn't wander, for 10 days. They reported that after 3 days, they were able to have a physical sensation without reacting to it, from a powerful urge to murder someone to an itch from a mosquito bite.

Ten minutes to begin with, will do.

Simply sit, as usual. On the floor with legs crossed, both feet or one foot resting on the opposite knee, or on a chair, in your usual sitting place, or anywhere you can be absolutely quiet and undisturbed. Close your eyes. Breathe slowly, deeply, naturally, in and out. Simply follow the breath. Focus on inhaling and exhaling, nothing else. You will feel your breath softly above your lips after a while. Feel nothing else but the air going in, coming out.

Your mind will wander off, into this or that thought, along this or that fantasy, plan, through the list of things you must do. Don't yank or scold. Just bring your focus gently back to the breath. In and out. In and out. Mind your back and keep it straight so the lungs are free to breathe properly.

You will begin to make some discoveries. That it is our own reactions to the outside world that create action, not the world itself. Watch your emotions, pain, pleasure, come and go. You will see nothing is permanent, none of those feelings lasts. Hatred, passion, greed, and their physical sensations come and go. Let them and their physical sensations pass without reaction. Just observation, as in, there's anger, there's anxiety, there's pleasure.

This silent focus on the breath is a marvelous opportunity to examine the inner country of one's own mind and its contents, its passions, its opinions, its urgencies.

Love: Not Self, Dependency, Thought, Or Image • 161

The prisoners said this kind of meditation, this kind of observation changed them from mean and miserable into people who can stand themselves.

We'd better pay some attention. We're all prisoners like them.

— • —

The development of our own cerebral cortex has resulted in the thrills of intellectual achievement...but can you imagine when the probe creatures from another civilization arrive how they'll react with horror at the mindless, hideous, primitive creatures they encounter here?

Fox Mulder
Field Report, X-Files

— • —

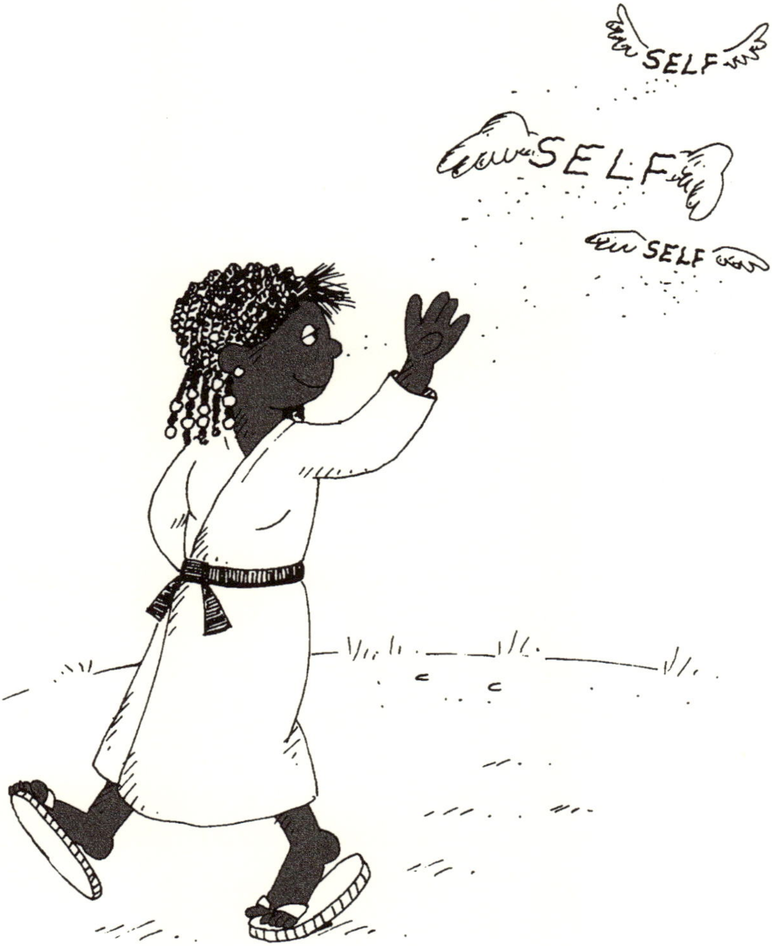
SELF
SELF
SELF

Truth, God, And Death

In a way, truth, god, and death are all the same. The truth is, as we've discovered, that the self, all that living according to the past, to blindly obeyed tradition, like a mechanical robot repeating over and over whatever it's been told, is the problem.

As you've discovered for yourself in quiet meditation, the death of the self, even its absence for a few seconds at a time, leaves only intelligence, truth, connection, love, goodness; in another word — life.

The body doesn't have to die for *you, your self with all the content of your consciousness,* to die.

Every time you've done a sitting as you've been reading this book, or when you've taken a walk alone, or sat without thinking of yourself with someone you love, or really listened to beautiful music, or really seen and touched a tree, or smiled good morning to a stranger, or picked up trash somewhere you don't have to, or taught someone younger than you to throw a ball or diaper a baby — whenever you've looked at the world or anyone in it *with new eyes* instead of old ideas — in those moments, your self has died and something else, whether you call it God or Love or the Spirit of the Universe, is *there.*

No matter how hard we try to fix it, whack at it, mold it, better it, refurnish it, give it different names, the self (and all its little selfs) is trouble. It is lonely, cut off, feels separate, no matter how many cars in the garage, no matter how much prestige it has. And it also doesn't matter how many teams it makes, how many friends it has, how good its grades, how cool its lover, how big its family, how industrialized its country. In the very act of making itself grand, it makes itself separate, lonelier than ever.

But there we are. Stuck with the self that the human brain invents.

Just seeing this to be truth makes our stuckness easier. At least we don't invest the self with more importance than it already feels.

When Jesus said, "Die to be born again," he knew what he was talking about. He may not have meant the death of the body comes before heaven, but the death of the self. You don't have to wait to die to reincarnate, as the Eastern religions suggest. You can reincarnate into a better place this afternoon.

As for physical death, the death of the body, what is it but a return of atoms to atoms? Everything is made of the same stuff in the universe, us and the trees and the stars. We, it all, came out of the big bang, when all the matter in the universe exploded out of a single density. Says Stephen Hawking, a physicist, cosmologist, and one of the great minds of the twentieth century, "There was a time, about ten or twenty thousand million years ago, called the big bang, when the universe was infinitesimally small and infinitely dense. Everything came from the exploding matter of that density, that ball of matter."

— • —

One may say that time had a beginning at the big bang, in the sense that earlier times simply would not be defined... One can imagine that God created the universe at literally any time in the past....the universe is expanding [objects like stars and galaxies, once close together, are observably flying apart from each other in the universe around us like spots on a balloon blowing up] and there may be physical reasons why there had to be a beginning...An expanding universe does not preclude a creator, but it does place limits on when he might have carried out his job!

Stephen W. Hawking
A Brief History of Time
From the Big Bang
To Black Holes

— • —

All creative minds, physicists, metaphysicists, thinkers of all kinds, respect the mystery of the universe, whatever name they give it. The human brain did not create a tree, or itself, for that matter, and that's that. Call whoever or whatever did create it all whatever you like.

Also, among our other thoughts, thought has invented the idea of death. There really isn't such a thing, only physical change we call death. When my five-year-old grandson Chaney asked me about it one day, death that is, I explained to him that since we are all made of stardust (and we are!) we simply turn back into stardust again (we do!). Whereupon, he picked up his shirt and stared down at his little belly in awe. I could see in his eyes, that he was looking into his belly at the stars. He is too young to worry about some thought-invention called a self.

So, once again, we're stuck on the business of the self. Some call it a soul, an Atman, a godhead, the Buddha in us. But what is it we want to go on living forever? This suffering self? This boring, frightened, petty, needy, little bundle of nerves?

Why not let it die now? And never fear death again.

I once asked a friend of mine, a physicist/metaphysicist in India, whether the self died or disappeared while I was paying attention in meditation. "Did it come back again?" asked Kishore. "If the self came back, clearly it didn't die for all time. But let it die as often as possible."

So. What we discover is that the truth is, nothing stays the same, everything changes. This is terrific if you're feel-

Truth, God, And Death • 167

ing bad, but scary if you like the way things are. Of course, even if you like the way things are, the human brain gets bored easily, so even sweet moments turn sour if they go on long enough. (If you don't believe this, as always, experiment. How long can you make a kiss last, even with someone you're crazy about, without getting hungry, wanting to yawn, or at least change the subject? You may like to run marathons, but even the rare hundred-mile runners have to stop or drop at some point. On the cheerful side, the ending of one thing is the exact moment the next thing begins, even if your shutter speed is too slow to catch the new image.

My favorite illustration that the great truth is, nothing ever dies, came from a science fiction movie, the original version of *The Incredible Shrinking Man*. In the movie, the hero was exposed to radiation while he was out in his boat. At home, he began to shrink, bit by bit, until his clothes, his house, his life became too large for him. Eventually, his cat chased him down into the cellar, where he nearly drowned in a few drops of water. He made his escape out onto the lawn, where even the mown grass was a jungle. He stared up at the universe, and remembered his science. It doesn't matter how infinitesimally small I get, he remembered: nothing in this universe disappears.

And then there was the song performed by The Byrds, words adapted from *The Bible, Book of Ecclesiastes*, music by Pete Seeger.

To everything (Turn, Turn, Turn)
There is a season (Turn, Turn, Turn)
And a time for every purpose, under heaven
A time to be born, a time to die
A time to plant, a time to reap
A time to kill, a time to heal
A time to laugh, a time to weep
To everything (Turn, Turn, Turn)
There is a season (Turn, Turn, Turn)
And a time for every purpose, under heaven
A time to build up, a time to break down
A time to dance, a time to mourn
A time to cast away stones, a time to gather stones together
To everything (Turn, Turn, Turn)
There is a season (Turn, Turn, Turn)
And a time for every purpose under heaven
A time of love, a time of hate
A time of war, a time of peace
A time you may embrace, a time to refrain from embracing
To everything (Turn, Turn, Turn)
There is a season (Turn, Turn, Turn)
And a time for every purpose under heaven
A time to gain, a time to lose
A time to rend, a time to sew
A time to love, a time to hate
A time for peace, I swear it's not too late....

Index

A

Addiction 12, 130, 140, 155
Alcohol xxiii, 71, 76, 115
Alcoholics Anonymous 71, 102
Ali
  Quotes 76
Alpert, Richard (Ram Dass) 61
  Quotes 6, 25, 132

Angelou, Maya 50
  Quotes 111
Anger 28, 30, 34, 59, 91, 107, 115, 126, 130, 134, 160
  Meditation for 93
  Quote on 97
Anxiety 4, 23, 46, 51, 52, 156, 160
Awareness xvi, xxiv

B

Bible, The 50, 61
  Quotes 6, 37, 75, 89, 118, 168
Bohm, David
  Quotes 141
Brain xv, xvi, xxii, xxiv, 3, 4, 7, 9, 10, 13, 14, 19, 22, 31, 33, 34, 46, 47, 49, 51, 52, 54, 58, 83, 85, 91, 108, 113, 116, 119, 120, 134, 138, 140, 144, 148, 151, 152, 164, 166, 168
Breath 44, 49, 51, 54, 58, 72, 75, 77, 85, 88, 96, 106, 110, 115, 131, 138, 159, 160
  Vipasana 159
Breathing 14, 36, 137, 140, 156
Buddha 29, 50, 62, 78, 119, 144, 166
  Quotes 17

C

Carlson, Hannah, M.Ed., C.R.C.
  Quotes 151
Carter, Chris (X-Files) 64, 161
Comfort, Alex 31
Conflict xvi, 5, 28, 37, 67, 151
Connection xv, 44, 53, 72, 78, 105, 110, 130, 133, 137, 158, 163
Conscience 116
Consciousness xxv, 7, 35, 109, 117, 163
Crime xxi, 5, 21

D

Death xxvi, 5, 60, 83, 86, 88, 163, 166
  Quote on 165
Dependency 92, 109, 155, 157, 158
Depression xxii, 76, 86, 100, 101, 127, 129, 130
Desire 4, 28, 33, 99, 102
  Meditation for 101
  Quote on 102
Dhammapada 62
Dream
  Quote on 64, 65

Drugs xxiii, 15, 29, 57, 71, 76, 130, 131
du Bois, W.E.B. 50

E

Education 21, 71, 86, 126, 147, 148
  Quote on 151, 152
Einstein 119
Epstein, Mark
  Quotes 17, 25, 128
Escape xxiii, xxvi, 3, 4, 15, 71, 137, 139
Evolution xv, 117

F

Failure xxi, 3, 23, 96, 123, 124, 126
  Meditation for 127
  Quote on 128
Fear xxiii, 4, 6, 9, 20, 21, 23, 28, 33, 37, 46, 58, 59, 78, 83, 91, 92, 96, 106, 115, 129, 130, 134, 144, 148, 166
  Meditation for 85
Fisher, Ray
  Quotes 152, 156

Freedom 3, 12, 29, 33, 38, 59, 71, 78, 119, 133, 151
  Quote on 97
Fromm, Erich
  Quotes 158

G

Galileo 119
Gita, Bhagavad 50
Giovanni, Nikki
  Quotes 97
God 5, 34, 54, 56, 66, 71, 72, 78, 116, 133, 144, 157, 163, 164
Goldstein, Joseph
  Quotes 66
Gould, Stephen Jay 117

H

Habit 4, 12, 14, 25, 71, 76, 84, 87, 88, 100, 106, 118, 134
Haldane, Richard Burdon 33
Happiness xvi, 6, 34, 36
  Quote on 6
Hawking, Stephen W.
  Quotes 165
Hindu 50, 51

Hittleman, Richard 63
Hughes, Langston
  Quotes 64

I

Indian Holy Man
  Quotes 141
Insight xxvi, 19, 22, 23, 25, 33, 35, 53, 66, 84, 133, 134, 138
Intellect 10, 19, 21, 22, 23, 35, 144, 161
Intelligence 10, 19, 20, 21, 22, 23, 24, 33, 66, 85, 109, 116, 134, 155, 163
Isolation 44, 105, 108, 130

J

Jesus Christ 29, 78, 119, 144, 164
  Quotes 6, 118
Joy xxi, 15, 36, 38, 100, 119, 146

K

Khairnar, Kishore 166
King, Martin Luther, Jr. 97

Koran, The
  Quotes 146
Krishnamurti, J. 29, 50, 62, 119
  Quotes 6, 37, 46, 73, 97, 111, 152, 157
Kung Fu 50, 63

L

Lama, Dalai 33, 36
Lee, Mark R.E. xvi-xvii
Loneliness xxiii, 14, 43, 46, 83, 88, 106, 108, 111, 129, 130, 131, 134, 139, 144, 155, 157, 158
  Meditation for 135
  Quote on 132
Longing 99, 100, 101, 102
  Meditation for 101
  Quote on 102
Love 3, 5, 15, 29, 57, 100, 106, 109, 133, 138, 139, 155, 164
  Meditation for 110, 159
  Quote on 111, 157, 158

M

Maharshi, Ramana
   Quotes 89
Mantra 46, 49, 51, 60, 61, 138
Maugham, Somerset 109
Meditation xv, xxiii, xxiv, 41, 72, 116, 134
   Quote on 6, 25, 37, 45, 55, 56, 66, 78
   Side effects 52, 56
   Use of 22, 85
   Ways to meditate 22, 29, 49, 50, 51, 53, 58, 60, 63, 75, 85, 88, 110, 134
     Salute to the Sun 101
     Stretch exercises 93
     Vipasana 159
   What is meditation? 4, 11, 17, 20, 25, 37, 43, 45, 46, 49
   Where, when, with whom 69, 72, 75, 89
Memory xv, 9, 28, 33, 34, 52, 57, 58, 84, 85, 91
Merton, Thomas
   Quotes 36
Mindfulness 51, 60

Mohammed 29, 144
   Quotes 146
Money 3, 20, 83, 86, 99, 143
Moses 144
Mother Teresa 144
   Quotes 65
Moving Meditations 60
Mulder, Fox
   Quotes 64, 161

N

Nature xv, 33, 34, 51, 60, 108, 141, 148, 185

O

Observe/Observation xv, 31, 33, 115, 116

P

Pain xxi, xxiv, xxvi, 3, 4, 5, 10, 29, 34, 46, 64, 85, 86, 96, 119, 129, 132, 133, 134, 139, 160
Pay Attention xxiii, 12, 29, 65, 78, 83, 152
Peace 3, 38, 45, 53, 135, 169
Persig, Robert M. 65
   Quotes 116

Power 78, 99, 111, 114, 119, 137, 139, 144, 146, 155, 156
Prayer 46, 51, 60, 61, 65, 75, 135, 138
Progress 117

R

Ram Dass 61
  Quotes 6, 25, 132
Reading Meditation 61
Reincarnation 164
Relationships xxii, 105, 107, 108
  Family 25, 76
  Friends 87
  Loving 3, 87, 106, 109, 110, 139, 156, 157
  Meditation for 110, 135
Relaxation Techniques 51, 54, 75, 85, 110
Religion 14, 32, 72, 75, 99

S

Salute to the Sun 101
School 21, 71, 86, 126, 147, 148

Self, the xxiv, 9, 13, 14, 15, 17, 22, 25, 28, 29, 33, 43, 47, 59, 66, 71, 78, 83, 89, 92, 102, 110, 115, 118, 119, 128, 129, 132, 139, 155, 158, 163, 164, 166
  Quote on 17
Self-Awareness 11, 17, 24, 25, 28, 33, 105, 113, 114, 118, 134
Self-Knowledge 11, 17, 24, 25, 28, 33, 105, 113, 114, 118, 134
Sex xxiii, 15, 29, 44, 57, 99, 102, 115, 137, 138, 139
  Quote on 141
Shame xxii, 83, 85, 92
Silence xvi, 45, 46, 59, 60, 65, 71, 72, 78, 89, 96, 102, 111, 120, 131, 135, 138
Sitting Meditation 53
Society 12, 21, 96, 123, 137, 146, 149
St. Francis
  Quotes 135
St. John of the Cross
  Quotes 102
St. Therese of Lisieux 62, 78

Stretch Exercises 93
Success 3, 20, 28, 96, 123, 126, 146, 148
   Meditation for 127
   Quote on 128
Suffering xxiv, xxvi, 5, 34, 59, 129, 130, 166
Survival xxvi, 7, 85, 148
Suzuki, Shunryu
   Quotes 55, 78

T

Tai Chi 50, 75
Teen Voices Magazine 77
The Song of God: Bhagavad-Gita 36
Thought xxiv, 4, 9, 10, 12, 20, 21, 23, 29, 31, 34, 35, 37, 43, 44, 45, 54, 56, 58, 66, 85, 92, 100, 102, 127, 130, 134, 141, 152, 157, 158, 160, 166
   Quote on 37
Trungpa, Chogyam
   Quotes 37, 58, 74
Truth xvii, 5, 21, 23, 24, 31, 37, 46, 54, 71, 108, 116, 118, 130, 144, 146, 153, 163, 166
   Quote on 37, 73
Twist Magazine 77
Tzu, Lao 29
   Quotes 118

U

Universe 6, 7, 15, 34, 43, 54, 59, 62, 66, 72, 78, 86, 105, 106, 116, 118, 119, 132, 134, 148, 152, 164, 165, 166, 168
Upanishads 61

V

Van Clief, Ron
   Quotes 56
Violence xxi, 21, 97
Vipasana 159
Vision Quest, Native American 75

W

Waking Up xvi, 1, 38, 78, 89

Walking Meditations 60
Wilson, Bill
　Quotes 102
Writing Meditation 64, 134

X

X-Files 64, 161

Y

Yoga 49, 50, 55, 58, 60, 63,
　69, 75, 138

Z

Zen
　Meditation 51, 63, 69

Bibliography And Suggested Reading

In this bibliography, only books especially interesting to teenagers are listed. Most of the people and works that are fundamental to understanding the nature of meditation (that is, paying attention to the nature of the self in daily life) have been mentioned in the text and quoted in the quotes: *The Bible, Old and New Testaments*; *The Koran*; *The Vedanta, The Gita,* translated by Christopher Isherwood, 1972; Lao Tzu's The *Way of Life (Tao)* translated by Witter Bynner, 1998; the Penguin 1973 edition of Buddha's teachings, *The Dhammapada*; *Zen Mind, Beginner's Mind*, Shunryu Suzuki, 1979.

All the works of J. Krishnamurti, especially those addressed particularly to education for the young and young adult such as *Letters to the Schools* (1985). Also *On Right Livelihood* (1992), *The First and Last Freedom* (1954), *Krishnamurti: Reflections on the Self*, edited by Raymond Martin (1997), *The Book of Life: Daily Meditations with Krishnamurti*, edited by R.E. Mark Lee (1995).

You will want to read a wide variety of meditation writings from African cultures, both East and West Indian cultures, Peruvian, Chinese, Japanese, Tibetan, the early Christian saints, the Jewish scholars, and books by scientists like Einstein, Hawking, Bohm, Comfort, whose work constantly suggests the connection of the human brain with the physical universe. Many of these writings, as well as work by scientists in the fields of neurobiology, psychology, sociology, anthropology have also informed this book. A favorite science writer is Stephen Jay Gould, *Full House*, 1996, for instance. Major sources for facts and statistics in this book were newspapers and magazines, government publications, almanacs, public television specials, and news broadcasts.

Many of the books listed have already been mentioned in text of this book.

Carlson, Dale. *Where's Your Head? Psychology for Teenagers*. Revised Edition. Madison, CT: Bick Publishing House, 1998.

Dass, Ram (Richard Alpert). *Journey of Awakening: A Meditator's Guidebook.* Revised Edition. New York: Bantam Books, 1990. This American psychologist is also a spiritual teacher who has studied and practiced meditation in its many paths of mantra, prayer, singing, visualization, and "just sitting" to movement meditations like tai chi — and suggests various paths to find a personal, suitable way for each person.

Epstein, Mark. *Going to Pieces Without Falling Apart.* New York: Broadway Books, 1998. A psychiatrist's discovery that Western psychology's emphasis on the strengthening of the self and the ego is deeply flawed. Happiness comes from the more Eastern, and Buddhist, understanding of letting go of the self and its inherent self-centered suffering.

Goldstein, Joseph, and Jack Kornfield. *Seeking the Heart of Wisdom: The Path of Insight Meditation.* Boston: Shambala, 1987. The many forms of meditation lead to quieting the brain so that insight can take place.

Hittleman, Richard. *Yoga: 28 Day Exercise Plan: 500 Step-by-Step Photographs.* New York: Bantam Books, 1980. Simple exercises. step-by-step instructions, photographs teach yogic secrets of breathing, concentration, muscle control, relaxation, resulting in relief from pain, freedom from stress, more energy, more focus.

J. Krishnamurti. *Meeting Life: Writings and Talks on Finding Your Path Without Retreating from Society.* San Francisco: Harper Collins, 1991. Perceptions and wisdom on love, society, death, self-censorship, relationships, solitude, meditation, fear, anger, relationship to society, the problems of youth.

Merton, Thomas. *New Seeds of Contemplation.* New York: New Directions, 1961. An exploration of the inner journey emphasizing that what we need, what we seek, is inside us all the time.

Persig, Robert M. *Zen and the Art of Motorcycle Maintenance: An Inquiry Into Values.* New York: Bantam Books, 1981. Not as easy to read as others on this list, but as father and son journey across the country by motorcycle, the father examines the relationship of technology, science, and our educational systems to true quality in living life.

Trungpa, Chogyam. *Meditation in Action.* Boston: Shambala, 1996. This Tibetan meditation master explores the ability to see clearly into situations and deal with them skillfully, going beyond formal practice into creative living without the self-consciousness of the ego. A brief manual, and to the point. Also check out Trungpa's *The Myth of Freedom: and the Way of Meditation.* Shambala, 1998.

Van Clief, Ron. *Manual of the Martial Arts: An Introduction to the Combined Techniques of Karate, Kung-Fu, Tae Kwon Do, and Aiki Jitsu for Everyone.* New York: Rawson Wade Publishers, Inc., 1981. Step-by-step, movement-by-movement postures in this manual show you how to move through this self-instructional course in various of the martial arts. Basic and advanced.

Directory of Meditation Centers, Retreats, And Teaching Groups

The following is a list of national centers that teach practices of quieting body and brain so that meditation in daily life is easier. Proper physical exercise, proper breathing, healthful eating, the integration of personal and social living, mindful attention to the self, nature, the universe, the connection of everything to everything, right living, these are teachings in many centers, foundations, institutes that follow. For local groups near you, call these national centers.

186 • Meditation Centers, Retreats, And Teaching Groups

BRAHMA KUMARIS WORLD SPIRITUAL ORGANIZATION
Church Center for the United Nations
777 United Nations Plaza
New York, NY 10017
(718) 565-5133

The Brahma Kumaris World Spiritual University now has nearly 2,000 branches in over 50 countries, and serves as a nongovernmental organization of the United Nations. It offers retreats, conferences, workshops, individual and group classes at all levels of spiritual practice. Meditation and counseling therapy are available for adults, young adults, and special groups: AIDS patients, the physically disabled, drug-and-alcohol dependent.

HIMALAYAN INSTITUTE
RR 1, Box 400
Honesdale, PA 18431
(717) 253-5551 — (800) 444-5772

Yoga and meditation for personal growth of the individual and for the sake of society, for better health, for self-awareness to attend to various aspects of mind, body, emotions, mental balance. Stress management, biofeedback, natural health care, workshops, retreats, meditation, yoga programs.

INTEGRAL YOGA INSTITUTE
227 West 13th St.
New York, NY 10011
(212) 929-0585

Yoga, breathing, relaxation, concentration, meditation, chanting, self-inquiry for every aspect of the individual: physical, emotional, social, intellectual, and spiritual. There are 27 national teaching centers, and yoga homes connected with the institutes at many branches.

KRISHNAMURTI FOUNDATION OF AMERICA
Box 1560
Ojai, CA 93024
(805) 646-2726

The world influence of the nonsectarian religious teachings and meditations of J. Krishnamurti is carried on by the work, the schools, the publications, of the international Krishnamurti Foundations in California, all over Europe, the Far East, Latin America, Australia, Hawaii, Russia, Africa. Associated with the foundations are schools, study centers, retreat centers for the young as well as adults. These were established for those who want to understand life and themselves, and how to live a meditative life in the world without running away or dropping out. Call, for books, schools, literature, membership, to receive Bulletins.

SELF-REALIZATION FELLOWSHIP
3880 San Rafael Avenue
Los Angeles, CA 90065
(213) 225-2471

Unites East and West in an understanding of the fundamental harmony of all religious paths, with temples, retreats, meditation centers around the world. Network of groups and individuals serving those in need, worldwide prayer circle, homestudy series of yoga and meditation, spiritual and humanitarian work. Write or call for free literature and further information.

THE THEOSOPHICAL SOCIETY IN AMERICA
PO Box 270
Wheaton, Il 60187
(312) 668-1571

This is a nonsectarian body of seekers after truth, a Brotherhood of Humanity, to study comparative religion, philosophy, and science, to practice and study meditation. There are more than 150 branches, study centers, and camps in the United States.

TWIN CITIES VIPASSANA COOPERATIVE
1911 South 6th Street
Minneapolis, MN 55424
(612) 332-2436

Meditation without dogma, ritual, or cultural trappings. Clear, continuous observation of different aspects of the mind-body process. With this observation come insights into connectedness.

LOCAL CENTERS, GROUPS, RETREATS, CAMPS, WORKSHOPS

Zen Centers, Prayer Centers, Shambala Training in Tibetan Buddhism, Moslem Groups, Christian Church Groups, Jewish Temple Groups, Hindu Vedanta Training, Yoga Schools and Centers, all kinds of Meditation Centers and Study Groups can be found locally for your area by checking your telephone books in the Yellow Pages, as well as by writing or calling this listing. There are camps, retreats, renewal centers, monasteries and convents, in all major and many smaller cities, associated with most temples, churches, and in many communities associated with local groups and schools. Do call first. Do ask for literature to make certain there are age-appropriate groups, need-appropriate groups, and ready transportation to get there if you want to go, and to leave if you want to leave.

BICK PUBLISHING HOUSE
PRESENTS
PSYCHOLOGY FOR TEENAGERS
Dale Carlson • Hannah Carlson, M.Ed., CRC
Completely Rewritten and Up-To-Date

Stop the Pain
Teen Meditations
Find out how to use your own ability for physical and mental meditation to end psychological pain.

224 pages, $14.95
ISBN: 1-884158-23-4

Where's Your Head?
Psychology For Teenagers
Christopher Award Winner. How to find out about your own personality—how it was formed, and what you can do about it. Illustrated, indexed.

320 pages, $14.95
ISBN: 1-884158-19-6

Girls Are Equal Too
The Teenage Girl's How-to-Survive Book
An ALA Notable Book. How a girl can become the person, the full-fledged and free human being, she was meant to be. Illustrated, indexed.

256 pages, $14.95
ISBN: 1-884158-18-8

AVAILABLE AT YOUR LOCAL BOOKSTORE FROM:
BOOKWORLD, BAKER & TAYLOR BOOK COMPANY, AND INGRAM BOOK COMPANY

BICK PUBLISHING HOUSE
307 Neck Road, Madison, CT 06443
Tel (203) 245-0073 • Fax (203) 245-5990

❑ Girls Are Equal Too .... $14.95   ❑ Stop the Pain $14.95
❑ Where's Your Head? $14.95

Name: _____

Address: _____
Please send check or money order (no cash). Add $3.50 S&H.

BICK PUBLISHING HOUSE
PRESENTS
CONFESSIONS OF A BRAIN-IMPAIRED WRITER

A Memoir By Dale Carlson

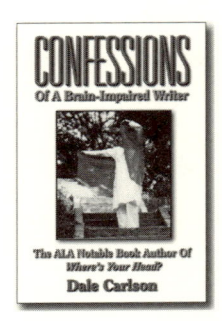

Writer, publisher, teacher, wife, mother, lover, wildlife rehabilitator and brain-impaired! A memoir.

Diagnosed gifted and learning disabled, at 59 she began the two ventures she was least qualified for and entered the "two Olympic events for which she had the least aptitude: a close relationship and a business." Her mental impairment creates havoc in her own life and the lives of others. She means no harm. She is as innocent of malice as any other natural disaster.

"*Confessions* is an important read for any person with a learning disability, or for anyone who…seeks to understand. Dale Carlson captures with ferocity the dilemmas experienced by people who have right hemisphere learning disabilties…she exposes the most intimate details of her life….Her gift with words demonstrates how people with social disabilities compensate for struggles with relationships."

— Dr. Kathleen C. Laundy, Psy.D., M.S.W., Yale School of Medicine

5-1/2 x 8-1/2, 224 pages
$14.95 paperback original
ISBN: 1-884158-24-2

AVAILABLE AT YOUR LOCAL BOOKSTORE FROM:
BOOKWORLD, BAKER & TAYLOR BOOK COMPANY, AND INGRAM BOOK COMPANY

BICK PUBLISHING HOUSE
307 Neck Road, Madison, CT 06443
Tel (203) 245-0073 • Fax (203) 245-5990
www.bickpubhouse.com

❏ Confessions of a Brain-Impaired Writer $14.95

Name: _____

Address: _____

Please send check or money order (no cash). Add $3.50 S&H.

BICK PUBLISHING HOUSE
PRESENTS
6 NEW BASIC MANUALS
FOR FRIENDS OF THE DISABLED
Hannah Carlson, M.Ed., CRC • Dale Carlson

Endorsed by Doctors, Rehabilitation Centers, Therapists, and Providers of Services for People with Disabilities

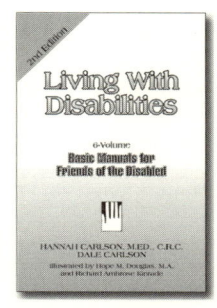

I Have A Friend Who Is Blind
ISBN: 1-884158-07-2, $9.95

I Have A Friend Who Is Deaf
ISBN: 1-884158-08-0, $9.95

I Have A Friend With Learning Disabilities
ISBN: 1-884158-12-9, $9.95

I Have A Friend With Mental Illness
ISBN: 1-884158-13-7, $9.95

I Have A Friend With Mental Retardation
ISBN: 1-884158-10-2, $9.95

I Have A Friend In A Wheelchair
ISBN: 1-884158-09-9, $9.95

Living With Disabilities 6-Volume Compendium
ISBN: 1-884158-15-3, $59.70

"Excellent, informative, accurate."
  - Alan Ecker, M.D.,
    Clinical Associate
    Professor at Yale

AVAILABLE AT YOUR LOCAL BOOKSTORE FROM:
BOOKWORLD, BAKER & TAYLOR BOOK COMPANY, AND INGRAM BOOK COMPANY

BICK PUBLISHING HOUSE
307 Neck Road, Madison, CT 06443
Tel (203) 245-0073 • Fax (203) 245-5990
www.bickpubhouse.com

- ❏ I Have A Friend Who Is Blind $9.95
- ❏ I Have A Friend Who Is Deaf $9.95
- ❏ I Have A Friend With Learning Disabilities $9.95
- ❏ I Have A Friend With Mental Illness $9.95
- ❏ I Have A Friend With Mental Retardation $9.95
- ❏ I Have A Friend In A Wheelchair $9.95
- ❏ Living With Disabilities $59.70

Name: _____

Address: _____

Please send check or money order (no cash). Add $3.50 S&H.

BICK PUBLISHING HOUSE
PRESENTS

7 BASIC MANUALS FOR WILDLIFE REHABILITATION
by Dale Carlson and Irene Ruth

Step-by-Step Guides • Illustrated • Quick Reference for Wildlife Care
For Parents, Teachers, Librarians who want to
learn and teach basic rehabilitation

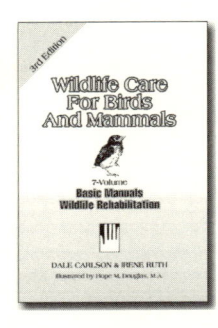

I Found A Baby Bird, What Do I Do?
ISBN: 1-884158-00-5, $9.95

I Found A Baby Duck, What Do I Do?
ISBN: 1-884158-02-1, $9.95

I Found A Baby Opossum, What Do I Do?
ISBN: 1-884158-06-4, $9.95

I Found A Baby Rabbit, What Do I Do?
ISBN: 1-884158-03-x, $9.95

I Found A Baby Raccoon, What Do I Do?
ISBN: 1-884158-05-6, $9.95

I Found A Baby Squirrel, What Do I Do?
ISBN: 1-884158-01-3, $9.95

First Aid For Wildlife
ISBN: 1-884158-14-5, $9.95

**Wildlife Care For Birds And Mammals
7-Volume Compendium**
ISBN: 1-884158-16-1, $59.70

Endorsed by Veterinarians, Wildlife Rehabilitation Centers, and National Wildlife Magazines

AVAILABLE AT YOUR LOCAL BOOKSTORE FROM:
BOOKWORLD, BAKER & TAYLOR BOOK COMPANY, AND INGRAM BOOK COMPANY

BICK PUBLISHING HOUSE
307 Neck Road, Madison, CT 06443
Tel (203) 245-0073 • Fax (203) 245-5990
www.bickpubhouse.com

- ❏ I Found A Baby Bird, What Do I Do? $9.95
- ❏ I Found A Baby Duck, What Do I Do? $9.95
- ❏ I Found A Baby Opossum, What Do I Do? $9.95
- ❏ I Found A Baby Rabbit, What Do I Do? $9.95
- ❏ I Found A Baby Raccoon, What Do I Do? $9.95
- ❏ I Found A Baby Squirrel, What Do I Do? $9.95
- ❏ First Aid For Wildlife $9.95
- ❏ Wildlife Care For Birds And Mammals $59.70

Name: _____

Address: _____

Please send check or money order (no cash). Add $3.50 S&H.

Author

Dale Carlson

Author of over fifty books, adult and juvenile, fiction and nonfiction, Carlson has received three ALA Notable Book Awards, and the Christopher Award. She writes novels and psychology books for young adults, and general adult nonfiction. Among her titles are *The Mountain of Truth* (ALA Notable Book), *Where's Your Head?* (Christopher Award), *Girls Are Equal Too* (ALA Notable Book), *Stop the Pain: Teen Meditations, Wildlife Care for Birds and Mammals*. Carlson has lived and taught in the Far East: India, Indonesia, China, Japan. She teaches writing and literature during part of each year. She lives in Connecticut with orphaned cats, raccoons, squirrels, and skunks.

Photo: Monica Feldak

Illustrator

Carol Nicklaus

Known as a character illustrator, her work has been featured in *The New York Times, Publishers Weekly, Good Housekeeping,* and *Mademoiselle*. To date she has done 150 books for Random House, Golden Press, Atheneum, Dutton, Scholastic, and more. She has won awards from ALA, the Christophers, and The American Institute of Graphic Arts.